# ON THE SECOND DAY OF CHRISTMAS

Published by Draft Horse Publishing
©Copyright 2020 by Deborah M. Hathaway
© 2020 Cover Art by Ashtyn Newbold
© Cover Photo by Martha Keyes

First Printed Edition, November 2020

ISBN 978-1-7334820-7-3

# ON THE SECOND DAY OF CHRISTMAS

DEBORAH M. HATHAWAY

# BOOKS BY DEBORAH M. HATHAWAY

Stand Alone Novels
A Secret Fire
When Two Rivers Meet
To Warm a Wintered Heart

*A Cornish Romance Series*
On the Shores of Tregalwen, a Prequel Novella
Behind the Light of Golowduyn, Book One
For the Lady of Lowena, Book Two
Near the Ruins of Penharrow, Book Three

*Belles of Christmas Multi-Author Series*
Nine Ladies Dancing, Book Four
On the Second Day of Christmas, Book Four

*Seasons of Change Multi-Author Series*
The Cottage by Coniston, Book Five

*For Chloe—*

*How lucky I am to have a niece*
*who loves reading*
*as much as I love writing.*

*Your support means the world to me.*
*Thank you!*

# CHAPTER 1

*ondon, December*
     Thick clouds cloaked the sky with an impenetrable grey, blocking out the warmth of the sun's light. The biting wind clipped through the London crowds, threatening to make good on its promise to undermine the scarves, gloves, and outerwear worn by those gathering on the frozen River Thames.

Despite the chill, the darkened skies, and the potential of even more snow, Miss Lucy Lincoln's enthusiasm would not be dulled. How could it be, now that this frigid winter had brought something as delightful as the Frost Fair to England?

She exited the carriage and neared the icy river, her eyes hungrily devouring the sight, as if the image would vanish if she didn't take it all in at once. Dull brown tents were pitched in rows across the ice, like giant animals lined up in a motionless caravan. Burgeoning snow had tipped a ship free of billowing sails onto its side near the tents, broken wood splintering from each end of the once-moving vessel.

A muted moodiness would have settled around the whole affair, were it not for the countless red and green cloaks and pelisses, the velvet bonnets decorated in holly and ivy, brightening the otherwise colorless imagery.

Lucy couldn't wait to add her own deep red pelisse to the masses. "Come along, Aunt Harriet. At this rate, all the good food and mementos will be gone before we even arrive."

Her aunt laughed at her side. "I assure you, there will be plenty of goods left for everyone. As for the food, you did see the size of the pig they are roasting, did you not? That is sure to feed the lot of us for weeks."

Aunt Harriet had already experienced the frozen Thames years ago, but this was Lucy's first, and she wouldn't waste a single moment of dallying.

She'd visited London more than a dozen times and often marveled at the size of the Thames. But now, with printing presses, tents, games, and hordes of people replacing the boats that had once roamed up and down the deep waters—it was the strangest sight Lucy had ever beheld.

They reached the outer edge of the river, and instead of pausing and warily eying the ice like the rest of the group, Lucy and Aunt Harriet strode forward without so much as a tentative step, marching confidently onto the uneven ice after paying a few coins for entrance.

Neither one of them had ever cowered from an adventure and walking across the frozen Thames would certainly be just that.

As they meandered past book stalls and drinking tents filled with laughter and smiles, Lucy's excitement buzzed within her. "Where shall we venture first, Aunt?"

"We must see it all, mustn't we?" White puffs of air lingered around Aunt from her words. "But first, that tantalizing smell of pork is calling to me."

Lucy grinned. "I was hoping you would say that."

With a shared look of enthusiasm, they traipsed across the river, following the thick scent of roasted mutton and pork. Finally, they neared the large fire blazing atop the ice, a full pig turning above the flames.

Grey smoke drifted to the even greyer skies, lingering above London and refusing to dissipate—like the smoke in Papa's library when he took to his pipe without opening the windows.

Mama would wander in with a wave of her hand and a scolding to her husband, though she always ended her words with a kiss atop his balding head. Papa would smile, then he'd return to reading whatever book had caught his fancy that day.

Lucy smiled at the memory. She hadn't seen her parents since leaving Northamptonshire at the beginning of the month and wouldn't be reunited with them until they made the journey themselves to London, hopefully before the end of Christmastide. She'd miss spending Christmas day with them this year, but then, had they come early with Lucy to Aunt Harriet's townhome in London, Lucy was fairly certain she would not have been allowed to go to the Frost Fair.

Mama and Papa had always encouraged her to make her own decisions, to be as free-spirited as Aunt Harriet—Mama's sister—but Lucy's parents themselves were far more reserved.

"Mama would not have approved of this, would she have, Aunt?"

They passed by a drinking tent filled with men and women alike. Beyond, a few young ladies slipped on the ice, falling softly on their backsides and revealing their stockings up to their knees. Instead of helping them up, a few men gawked with greedy eyes.

"No, she most certainly would not have approved," Aunt Harriet said. "Although, she would have been more inclined to take part in all of this when she and I were younger."

Lucy tipped her head. She couldn't imagine Mama stepping a single foot near such a place. But then, Aunt had often spoken of how Mama was as a child—as carefree and spontaneous as Aunt Harriet still was.

A flicker of sadness crossed Aunt's features before she returned her smile. "But no matter. I suppose we shall simply have to do something perfectly acceptable after this so she doesn't disapprove of us entirely. Perhaps visit a local bookshop? There's a lovely one not too far from here overlooking the river. Barrington Books."

A bookshop? Since when had Aunt Harriet ever wished to enter a bookshop? Lucy had always enjoyed reading, just like Papa, but Aunt could certainly not claim the same interest.

3

"Your father prefers reading about adventures to actually experiencing them," Aunt would often say in his presence with barely restrained derision.

Father, unaffected, would smile to himself and merely continue reading.

It was no secret Aunt Harriet and Father were polar opposites, or that Aunt disapproved of him. But each time she made some criticism of Papa, as little as it may be, irritation scratched at Lucy's nerves. Mama was happy with her husband—and Lucy with her father. Was that not enough for Aunt Harriet?

Before Lucy could ask such a thing, her ears perked at the sound of a thick French accent spoken nearby.

"You are certain it is safe, Lady Kirtley?" the young Frenchwoman asked. Her brownish-red ringlets draped past her temples as she peered disparagingly at the ice she stood upon.

An older woman stood beside her with an encouraging nod. "Yes, Miss Babineaux. It is perfectly safe."

The pretty Miss Babineaux hardly looked convinced, but her companion continued urging her until their small party disappeared into a nearby tent that played host to the distinct smell of mutton.

"Your parents would be just as frightened as that poor girl on the ice," Aunt Harriet said as Miss Babineaux disappeared within the mutton tent. "Thank heavens you are with me instead of her."

Lucy couldn't have said it better herself. She smiled, setting aside her earlier frustrations with Aunt as they moved forward.

"Have you come to eat, ladies?" A large man with a jolly smile and a round girth reached his arms out from side to side, as if welcoming them with an embrace. He continued shouting, despite their proximity to his nearby tent that brimmed with smoke from a cooking pig. "Do join the feast! Years from now, you shall be able to say that you've indulged in the best meal upon the Thames!"

Without hesitation, Lucy and Aunt Harriet entered the tent, taking a seat and accepting a large serving of roasted pork and boiled potatoes. The flag above the tent whipped against the wind with an occasional crack, but the loud laughter and conversation within the fabric walls of the tent sounded above all other noises.

No, her parents would not have approved of any of this.

But Lucy did. Thank heavens, indeed, for Aunt Harriet. The woman had always been more like a sister to Lucy than a guardian. With a mere fifteen years between them, the two of them had been known to become entangled often in predicaments—including becoming lost in Sherwood Forest because they insisted they knew the way better than their driver. They'd also nearly drowned in a boat on Lake Windermere because they told their guide they could row themselves when neither of them had before.

Lucy smiled as she bit into another piece of pork, her mouth flooding with moisture. Yes, she and Aunt Harriet were quite a handful when they were together. Fortunately, they always seemed to pull themselves out of whatever quandaries in which they involved each other.

But they certainly wouldn't find themselves in any trouble at a Frost Fair. There were plenty of constables present, the ice was sturdy, and Aunt would ensure they stayed away from the more questionable locations. With such safety measures in practice, her parents would be sure to understand why Lucy just had to attend.

After finishing "one of the best pieces of roasted pork I've ever tasted," Aunt Harriet led the way from the tent, and she and Lucy forged their way down the Thames—just as the boat they'd ridden in last summer had once done.

A large group of young men and women gathered together, dancing—and slipping—a reel to the lively tune created by fiddles.

Aunt Harriet motioned toward them. "Care to join?"

Lucy shook her head. She was all for being spontaneous and adventurous when it suited her, but she didn't do well in large groups of people whom she didn't know. It always made her nervous, and when she was nervous, she ran her tongue like a dog smacking his gums after eating honey.

They moved past printing presses—"purchase the poems for proof that you walked on the Thames!"—and booths filled with overpriced goods most people typically would not purchase. Since they were on the Thames, though, the vendors filled their pockets and purses with coins quickly.

As Aunt wandered a short distance away to another peddler, Lucy eyed a few pearl earrings before footsteps thumped behind her.

"Miss Lincoln!" A man's arms slipped round her waist, lifting her feet from the ground and spinning her above the ice.

She would have yelped had she not instantly recognized the tone.

"Martin Carter, you put me down this instant!" Her words sounded far lighter than she'd intended them as she ended them in a giggle.

With her feet once more settled on the ice, she whirled around to face her friend, ignoring the questioning and disapproving glances from others.

"I am so pleased to see you! It's been far too long. Months! I didn't think you would arrive, what with the weather we've been experiencing of late."

He flashed a charming grin, one that made other women swoon. One that only testified of Lucy's wise decision to remain solely friends with such a flirt.

"I wouldn't have missed Christmas in Town for the world!" he exclaimed. "Though that fog was simply shocking, wasn't it? Had I left Northamptonshire any later, I would've been locked indoors with my parents for all of Christmastide."

"And that would've been so very bad?"

"You know my parents, Miss Lincoln." He took on a high-pitched tone, mimicking his mother. "Martin, when will you provide me with grandchildren? Martin, why can't you simply choose *one* female with whom to flirt? Martin, you are the reason I shall die young."

He gave a theatrical sigh as Lucy laughed. "Your impression is uncanny."

And it was. Having grown up alongside the Carters, Lucy knew all too well how Mrs. Carter wished for her son to marry and how his father wished for an heir to his estate. When Martin Carter would return home from school, he would often share his frustrations over his parents with Lucy. He and Lucy had always gotten along well together, having quite similar personalities.

But where her own parents encouraged her to embrace her differences from other people, the Carters very much wished for their son to fit in with Society more than to stand out.

"Being around them is exhausting," Mr. Carter continued. "But in London, I am free to be with whomever I wish."

His gaze roved over to where two ladies eyed him from across the way. He winked, and they giggled, scurrying past him.

Lucy watched with amusement. "Mmm, yes. And you are free to be with them for however long—or short—you wish." She quirked a knowing brow.

Mr. Carter grinned. "That's the beauty of being a charismatic gentleman, I suppose. Although, in truth, my bachelorhood may be coming to an end."

"Oh?" That was surprising news, indeed. Mr. Carter had never once expressed a desire to wed. Had he finally found a woman to change his mind? "And why is that?"

Before he could respond, Aunt Harriet appeared beside Lucy. "Mr. Carter, how do you do?"

Mr. Carter bowed, reaching forth to place a quick peck to Aunt Harriet's gloved hand. "Mrs. Bird, you are still as lovely as any woman I have ever known. Though your niece inches closer by the day."

Lucy and Aunt were both well aware of Mr. Carter's tendency to flirt with whomever he pleased. Even still, his flattery somehow managed to make them both giggle behind their gloves.

"You are looking rather lively yourself, Mr. Carter," Aunt said.

"A little ruddy in the cheeks but overall healthy," Lucy teased.

"I'm glad you think so," he said with a wink. "But who could help looking so lively with such a festivity as this?" He waved his arms around him. "Such a wonderful thing, is it not? I'm glad the both of you have decided to join in the fun. Though, I should've known neither of you would let anything stop you from enjoying yourselves."

"Never," Lucy and Aunt Harriet replied at the same time.

Mr. Carter chuckled, rubbing his gloved hands together. His lips were tight, as if frozen stiff from the cold. "Well, I would love to stay and chat with you both, but I've promised to join in a game of skittles near the Blackfriars Bridge. You'd both be welcome to watch if you'd like." He raised a brow at Lucy. "I know how you enjoy observing me when I play."

Lucy feigned a scoff. "Oh, do go on before you charm us half to death."

"I will call upon you soon, yes? Lovely to see you both again!" After a bow of departure, he bounded as carefully as possible across the ice.

Lucy watched after him with a humored sigh, but Aunt Harriet's gaze remained on Lucy.

# CHAPTER 2

"What is it?" Lucy asked.

Aunt Harriet walked ahead without a word, focusing on the booths they passed. Lucy knew what Aunt had been about to say, and though she wished to set it aside, the unspoken words wedged beneath her nerves in a way she could not bear.

"Aunt, we've been through this before."

Aunt Harriet sighed. "I know we have. And I won't say another word on the matter. Only..." She paused near a booth filled with books. Instead of looking at the novels, however, she peered across at Lucy. "Only I fear no matter how often we speak of this, I will never understand why you will not marry the man." She lowered her voice. "And I do not say such things lightly. You know how I feel about marriage, my dear."

Lucy nodded. How could she forget? After Aunt Harriet's miserable marriage ended due to the sudden illness and premature death of her husband, nearly all of England knew the woman had vowed to never marry again.

Aunt Harriet reached forth, grasping Lucy's hands in hers. "I would never wish a union upon anyone, and that is a fact."

"Yes, Aunt, but I—"

She held up a finger. "But you *do* wish to marry, so I will support you in your decision."

Lucy's chest tightened. Despite the reassuring words, disappointment laced throughout Aunt Harriet's tone. Lucy wanted to please her, but no matter how she tried to change her own feelings, she could not shake the desire she had to one day marry and have a family of her own.

Still, to know she was displeasing Aunt Harriet wasn't a feeling that she wished to linger. "I am sorry, Aunt."

"Oh, there is no need to apologize. Above all else, I wish for your happiness—for you to find a husband who does not snuff out that free spirit you have—as my husband did to me. As your—" She ended abruptly, shaking her head with a sigh. "It would be a most terrible life to live."

Lucy narrowed her eyes. What had Aunt been about to say?

"You trust me, do you not, Lucy?"

Setting her curiosity aside, Lucy nodded. She recalled the change that had come over Aunt Harriet the moment the mourning period had ended a decade ago for her departed spouse, Uncle Francis. The light had returned to her eyes after being absent for ten years of marriage. That alone was enough to convince Lucy to choose her husband carefully, because despite Aunt Harriet's unfortunate union, Lucy still had hope that she herself would find a gentleman worthy of her love.

"Excellent," Aunt Harriet continued, her brown eyes sparkling. "Then I have decided that I shall be the one to help you in your quest to find the perfect gentleman. And my first choice for you would have to be—now do not protest so very greatly, as you have done before—Mr. Carter."

"Aunt," Lucy began with another sigh. She'd heard this argument countless times before. Truly, this was one of the many instances where she preferred her parents to Aunt Harriet. They may not be as adventurous, but at least they were nowhere near as stubborn or headstrong as Aunt.

"No, no, you must listen to my reasoning," Aunt Harriet continued.

"He is charming, he gets along superbly with your family, and he is so very wealthy. Most importantly, he is as spontaneous and adventurous as the both of us. He surely would allow you to be as wild as you desire. He is also—"

"Not in love with me." Lucy stared pointedly at her aunt. "Nor am I in love with him."

Aunt pursed her lips in what could only be considered an adult pouting. Lucy smiled. "I am sorry to dampen your hope, but truthfully, it cannot happen. We've known each other for years. I know of his many virtues. But there is nothing beyond friendship between the both of us, I assure you."

With a sigh, Aunt stepped past the book booth. "Love." She said the words with a flair of her nostrils. "If only our hearts could be controlled."

"Indeed."

"And if only you could fall in love with him as easily as you flirt with him." With an airy sigh, Aunt Harriet stepped away. "Now, let us see what all the fuss is about with these printed papers."

She stepped toward one of the presses nearby, but Lucy didn't follow. Of course Aunt Harriet hadn't meant her words to be taken cruelly. But the words had already rooted in Lucy's conscience.

*As easily as you flirt with him.*

Lucy hadn't been accused of being too flirtatious for four years, ever since...

No. She shook her head. She didn't wish to think of such things. Not at the Frost Fair.

After all, she'd grown over those four years and had learned a great many things—especially not to flirt with just any gentleman. Besides, she and Mr. Carter had discussed their relationship a number of times. They were close friends, and close friends they would remain. As for their flirting, it was mutual and perfectly harmless.

Her brow pursed. Of course, she'd been wrong about that before. When...when she'd wounded poor little Benjamin Kent.

She cringed, unable to stop her thoughts from continuing. He was always such a sweet boy. Though he was six years Lucy's senior, she'd often thought of him as younger than her, what with his shy tendencies and small frame when he was a boy. Of course, he'd grown into his shoulders eventually. But had she any notion Mr. Kent had loved her as much as he did, she never would have given him false hope in the form of flirtatious remarks. She never would have...

She blew out a frustrated puff of air that floated around her in a cloud. She'd told herself not to dwell on him. Four years had passed. The regret should have fled by now. After all, he was sure to have moved on from what had happened. She'd heard that he'd even finished his study of medicine and now had his own practice.

But she would think no more of the man. For whether he had moved on or not, the thought of merely interacting with him again was just too much to bear.

Especially after what she did to him.

"Lucy, look! Mince pies."

Lucy blinked, coming out of her reverie. Aunt Harriet pointed across the way to where a man walked with a large basket in his arms, filled full of mince pies.

"Oh, that would be just the thing to warm us, would it not?" Aunt Harriet said.

Lucy grinned. The both of them had weaknesses for pork *and* pies.

"I'll catch up to him alone," Lucy said. "That way you may purchase a few prints for us."

She winked at her beaming aunt then scurried off to catch the mince pies before the man wandered too far away.

"Best mince pies on the River Thames!" he shouted. "Tell your children of the time you ate the best mince pies on the River Thames!"

"Lucy?"

She turned around at Aunt Harriet's call, walking backwards and still progressing through the crowds.

"You must purchase more than one for me, mind!"

Lucy laughed. "But of course! I wouldn't think to—"

"Lucy!" Aunt's eyes widened. "Watch your—"

But the warning came too late. The heel of Lucy's boot hit against something solid, and she flew backward, yelping just before she landed hard against a pile of gathered snow. The breath rushed from her lungs, and her head bounced roughly against the packed snow.

"Lucy!" cried her aunt's voice somewhere in the distance.

Pain rocked through Lucy's body, her lungs aching as she tried to breathe. More shouting occurred, and soon Aunt Harriet spoke from her side. "Oh, my dear Lucy. Please tell me you are well."

Lucy tried to respond, but only a groan emerged from her lips, the pulsing in her head making her eyes spin.

"Is she all right?" a voice asked nearby.

"Fetch a physician!" cried another.

"Oh, please be well!"

"I'm a physician."

A calm voice rose above the turmoil.

A *familiar* voice, though one Lucy could not place.

Her eyes flickered open, but her blurred vision made her stomach turn, and black spots appeared before her. She was acquainted with this feeling of losing consciousness. She'd experienced the same thing when she'd fallen from a low branch of a tree as a little girl, climbing it with Aunt Harriet when Uncle Francis had been away for a few weeks.

"Please, help her." Aunt Harriet's voice sounded muffled, as if spoken from across the river of ice and not right beside Lucy.

"Worry not, ma'am."

There was that voice again, that soothing, calming voice. The voice that made her feel as if she sat before a crackling fire, a warm blanket across her lap as snow fell gently outside. The voice that tempted her to give in to the darkness that closed in with every passing second.

But when frigid fingers touched her cheeks, she was jarred awake. Her eyes flew open, and she focused on the stranger hovering above her, peering directly into her eyes.

Only, he was no stranger.

"Mr. Kent?" she breathed, trying to focus on his features, though her eyes blurred once again.

Had she conjured him from her musings only moments before?

His lips twitched, his cold fingers still against her cheek. "Lie still, Miss Lincoln."

"You know my niece?" Aunt Harriet sounded closer, but Lucy's head took to spinning again.

Mr. Kent—*Dr.* Kent—needn't tell her to lie still. She wouldn't have moved even if she'd wanted to, for she was rendered motionless from utter shock.

She held her breath unwittingly, more black spots speckling her vision until she closed her eyes. This time, Benjamin Kent's cold fingers didn't shock her back to consciousness. This time, she welcomed the darkness—for with it, she could finally hide from her shame in knowing already that this man would care for her, even after all she had done to him.

# CHAPTER 3

*B*enjamin Kent shifted on his knees beside Miss Lucy Lincoln—Lucy Lincoln, of *all* people. He reached into his waistcoat pocket, pulling out his smelling salts and flipping open the lid to wave the pungent odor beneath her slightly turned-up nose.

When he'd first spotted Miss Lincoln near the tents, he'd swiftly made up his mind to avoid the woman at all costs. But when she'd recklessly run backwards and tripped on an uneven ledge of ice, Benjamin could not, in good conscience, keep away.

He was a physician first and foremost. No matter their history. No matter how he'd spent the last four years of his life trying to forget her and her actions toward him. He had a duty to perform.

He placed the salts under Miss Lincoln's nose again. In another moment, she gasped, her eyes flying wide open. Her gaze darted around haphazardly before she winced, raising a hand to cover her eyes.

She could move her limbs without protest. That was a good sign.

Blasted Frost Fair. Whoever's fool idea it was to hold a fair on an icy river ought to be the one helping the injured. He'd already seen to two women and a child who'd fallen earlier that morning—and he knew he'd see to many more in the future.

He turned to Miss Lincoln's Aunt, Mrs. Bird. "Did you arrive here by carriage?"

"Yes, of course."

"Then I suggest Miss Lincoln be transported home immediately."

Mrs. Bird pumped her head up and down. "I'll send for my groom and footman to help."

As she hailed a nearby gentleman to retrieve her servants, Benjamin faced the woman still lying on the piled up snow. "Miss Lincoln, can you hear me?"

She mumbled a barely coherent, "Yes."

"Do you remember what has just happened?"

Mrs. Bird returned her attention to Miss Lincoln, kneeling down at her opposite side with a wary eye on Benjamin. No doubt she still wondered how he knew her niece. He wasn't about to remind the middle-aged woman that she, herself, knew him as well. They'd only met *three* times.

He ignored the irritation inching up his spine. Wild emotions would not do when a woman's health was at risk. "Miss Lincoln?" he pressed.

The young woman groaned, shifting in the snow, clearly disoriented. "I…I believe I fell."

Her words were slightly slurred—indicative of a head trauma. But the injury was only slight if she could remember how she'd obtained it. "Can you tell me if you are experiencing any pain?"

Her eyes fluttered open again, but this time, her gaze fell on him. After a dazed blink, recognition dawned in her brown eyes as clearly as the sun breaking through a chilled, morning mist over a freshly plowed field.

She'd already recognized him before, but instead of losing consciousness again, Miss Lincoln merely covered her eyes with a gloved hand, releasing another groan.

She was mortified at seeing him. There was no other explanation for it. But was she merely embarrassed because of her fall—or because she had sprouted a conscience sometime in the last four years and now felt remorse for what she had done to him?

How he could only hope for the latter. How he knew it would only be the former.

"Are you injured elsewhere, Lucy?" Mrs. Bird gently prompted when Miss Lincoln remained silent.

With her eyes still covered, she shook her head. "Only the back of my head."

Benjamin faced Mrs. Bird. "I must see if she's bleeding, ma'am. If you might help to remove her bonnet?"

Mrs. Bird went straight to work untying Miss Lincoln's ribbon beneath her chin, her fidgeting fingers revealing her nerves. In a matter of moments, Benjamin was able to slip his own calm hand underneath Miss Lincoln's head.

Past the coiffure and smooth curls, there was no excess moisture, despite the very large bump forming just below the crown of her head.

He withdrew his hand—untainted by any hint of blood—and faced her aunt once again. "Mrs. Bird, I don't believe there's any cause for grave concern as of right now, but..." He paused, drawing in a deep breath for what he knew he needed to say, though it was the last thing he wished to do. "I need to conduct a full examination of her wound, if only to be certain."

"Yes, yes, of course. We're situated on Grosvenor Street." Mrs. Bird glanced back distractedly as her servants finally appeared. Crinkled brows and lowered lips twisted both men's features. "We must help Miss Lincoln to the carriage. She has suffered a fall and hit her head."

At once, the men went into action, and Benjamin stepped back more than happily. He wasn't about to suggest *he* carry the young woman to her carriage. No doubt she would have laughed at his offer —like she'd done four years ago at an entirely *different* offer he'd made.

"Mrs. Bird," he began, if only to stop his thoughts, "I will follow you shortly."

After simple instructions on how to help Miss Lincoln before he arrived, Benjamin bade farewell with a tip of his hat just as the able-bodied groom hoisted Miss Lincoln from the ground.

Turning his back to them, Benjamin drew a deep breath and shook out his hands, relief flooding him to have a moment away from the woman.

Perhaps he ought to request another doctor to take over for him. Dr. Mason would be more than happy to have another client, what with his new practice. Benjamin wasn't one to easily give up on his patients, but Miss Lincoln was no mere patient. There was too much between them for him to continue on.

*Think of the money, Benjamin.*

He blew out a sigh, walking past men with their boisterous laughter as they played skittles, ladies giggling empty-headedly as they watched them.

Benjamin wasn't scrapping for money, by any means. In fact, he lived more comfortably now than he ever had before. There were still things he wished to do though, namely provide a better living for his parents and soon set up a practice near the sea, far away from the bustle of Town.

Mrs. Bird would be sure to pay handsomely, like most wealthy, female guardians. He may as well take advantage of the opportunity, even if that meant being around Miss Lincoln a time or two more.

Besides, he had a desire to know if she did, indeed, feel remorse for her treatment of him. Not that it mattered so very greatly, of course. He'd overcome much in his life—poverty, loneliness, cruelty… rejection. He could handle a small, professional visit with Miss Lincoln.

Most especially because he was indifferent toward the woman, and indifferent, he would remain.

After retrieving his medical bag, he made straight for Grosvenor Street. Upon his arrival, he was greeted with a hasty welcome then quickly ushered to the upper floor, where he waited outside of Miss Lincoln's room.

His stomach shifted as the maid slipped through the door to ensure Miss Lincoln was ready to be examined. Why his stomach turned again was beyond him. He'd performed countless examinations with countless patients in the last four years—and he'd worked hard to establish his own practice.

Miss Lincoln was just another young woman.

And yet, when he was finally shown into her room, his wits dimmed faster than the embers floating up from the crackling fire in the hearth before her bed.

Miss Lincoln lay beneath a thick, crimson cover, her blonde curls sprawled and crinkled across her white-as-snow pillow. Her bonnet, pelisse, and dress had been removed and replaced with her white shift and green, floral dressing gown.

Seeing the woman in such a state should not have affected Benjamin. And yet, he was as unraveled as his mother's spool of thread that he'd allowed a stray cat to play with when he was a boy.

He should not be feeling this way. He should not be feeling *any* way. Where had his common sense fled?

"Come in, Dr. Kent."

Benjamin snapped to attention as Mrs. Bird waved him closer, sitting at the edge of Miss Lincoln's bed. Miss Lincoln merely kept her arm draped over her eyes.

He stepped fully into the room, gathering his unpleasant memories of the girl as inefficiently as one would gather errant snowflakes falling from the sky. He strode across the room with squared shoulders and a raised chin.

"How are you feeling, Miss Lincoln?" He placed his medical bag on the table beside her bed.

She didn't move. For a moment, he wondered if she'd feign sleeping, but she responded in a whisper, her arm still covering her eyes.

"My head still aches."

"That is to be expected after the fall you took."

He moved next to the wash basin he'd requested from Mrs. Bird earlier. Many of his own colleagues didn't see the value in proper cleanliness, but after four years of practicing, Benjamin had seen the clear advantage of keeping his hands and tools clean—for the benefit of himself and his patients.

After drying his washed hands on a fresh towel, he faced Miss Lincoln once again. "In order to ensure your injury is not so very grave, I will ask you a series of questions. Will that be all right with you, Miss Lincoln?"

"Yes," she whispered.

He returned to his bag, pulling out a small booklet and a pencil. "Can you tell me your name?"

She shifted against her mattress. "Lucy Harriet Lincoln."

Mrs. Bird looked to Benjamin with a hopeful expression. He nodded reassuringly then focused once more on his paper. "And what is your day of birth?"

"The twenty-fourth of February, seventeen ninety-two."

"And your parents' names?"

For the first time since he'd arrived, she peeked at him from beneath her cover, though her eyes were hardly visible in the shade her arm cast. "Henry and Emma Lincoln."

"Do you remember what you were doing before you fell?"

Finally, she removed her arm. Mrs. Bird took the opportunity to replace the cloth across Miss Lincoln's brow with a fresh, damp one. "I was running for a few mince pies when I walked backwards and tripped on the ice."

Mrs. Bird winced. "I never should've mentioned those pies to you, my dear. This is my fault."

"This is in no way your fault, Aunt. It was my own recklessness, as usual." Miss Lincoln delivered a weakened smile before closing her eyes again.

Benjamin watched the exchange with as much disinterest as possible. Were he an outsider looking in, he would've admired their relationship, their obvious camaraderie.

But Miss Lincoln had been correct in her analysis. She *was* being reckless. Reckless and spontaneous and headstrong—typical behavior of the young woman, especially when she was around Mrs. Bird.

Echoes of past words coasted around his mind like wayward robins lost in a storm.

*"I would travel the world if my dear aunt insisted upon it!"*

*"I've never known someone I admire so much as Aunt Harriet."*

*"I must marry someone who will not impede my desire to be as free-spirited as I am—as my dear aunt always tells me. I fear you* would *impede my spirit, Mr. Kent."*

Benjamin flinched. Embarrassment—that ugly emotion he'd worked so hard to squelch—reared its brazen head like an untamed stallion.

He clenched his teeth, striving to rein in the feral animal. "Very well, Miss Lincoln. I have one more question for you."

*Do not say it, Benjamin. Do not unearth the past you worked so hard to bury.*

But logic fled. The beast escaped his clutches and pushed the words straight from his mouth, desperate for validation—desperate for an apology.

"Do you remember the last time we met together?"

Miss Lincoln's eyes jumped to his, wide and clear. Mrs. Bird, unaware of the change of state in her niece, turned to squeeze out the moisture from another rag. The woman clearly had no notion of Benjamin's request of her niece four years ago.

Miss Lincoln, however, did.

She opened her mouth, but no sound escaped from it.

"It is a simple question, Miss Lincoln. Do you remember, or do you not?"

He strengthened his stare, willing her to admit to what had happened between them—at least mentally. He ought not press her, what with her recent injury. But four years of his own repressed emotions rushed past the weirs and flooded his entire being.

Finally, she nodded. Her eyebrows raised, moisture glistening in her brown eyes, and her voice as quiet as a draft of wind. "Yes. Yes, I do remember."

Instead of validating his emotions, that draft-of-wind whisper slipped through the cavities of his chest and cut his heart with frozen slashes. Why had he brought up the painful memory? Did he expect an apology? A reasoning for her poor treatment of him?

No matter what she said, nothing could erase the damage she'd done to his heart.

As Mrs. Bird returned with another rag for Miss Lincoln's brow, Benjamin finally looked away, jotting a few notes into his book.

When Miss Lincoln was nervous—which was not very often—she used to prattle away like a child, unable to curb her tongue. Had she grown out of such a habit, or was she really unaffected by his blunt words?

"Your memory seems unaffected by your fall." His voice was hard—much harder than he'd intended. "But I should like to listen to your heart and lungs all the same."

In truth, he *wouldn't* like to. Not in the slightest. But he'd never forgive himself for performing half of a job with a patient. Even *if* that patient was Lucy Lincoln.

After ensuring her reflexes worked properly and that she had feeling in each of her limbs, Benjamin waited for Mrs. Bird to help Miss Lincoln sit upright in bed.

Typically, he'd listen to his patients' lungs and heart by pressing his head to their chest. With young women, it was far more proper for him to listen to such things by way of their backs.

Even still, being so close to Miss Lincoln, leaning his head against her thin dressing gown and actually focusing on the sound of her lungs and heartbeat, took more willpower than he wished to admit.

He'd imagined being so near this woman for half his life growing up, longing to share his future with her. But now his stomach twisted at their proximity.

"Breathe deeply for me," he instructed, his voice raspier than he would have preferred as his jaw brushed against the dressing gown.

She obeyed, and the warmth of her skin seeped through her garment onto his cheek until he could no longer bear it.

He pulled away with rattled nerves, moving next to feel the back of her head. The bump had already grown, but elsewhere, the swelling was fortunately absent.

After performing his duties, he swiftly retreated across the room to the wash basin.

The cold water was sure to do him good.

"It is a sizable injury, and you will be bruised for a few days, but as of right now, I don't believe there is anything to be overly concerned about."

As Mrs. Bird helped Miss Lincoln to lie back on the bed, Benjamin scrubbed the numb feeling from his fingers that had somehow occurred due to the absurd softness of the woman's too-blonde curls.

Miss Lincoln resumed her position with her arm over her eyes. That was more than fine with Benjamin. He'd simply relay the rest of the information to Mrs. Bird.

"I'll leave you with a prescription for the apothecary. Included will be a few things that will take away most of the pain she'll be feeling for a day or two, as well as a sleeping draught to help her throughout the night. I urge you to keep her abed for at least two days. If she improves, she may resume simple activities as time progresses."

"You will come back to check on her tomorrow?" Mrs. Bird asked expectantly. "I would have my own physician do so, but I feel far more comfortable with you, as you've seen to her from the beginning."

She flashed him a charming smile—one that had been absent each time he'd met her prior. The Lincolns—Mr. and Mrs. Lincoln, to be exact—had always been more than kind to Benjamin and his family. Mrs. Bird, however, never had time for the son of an apothecary, but now that Benjamin was a respected physician, she could treat him with kindness. Was that also why Miss Lincoln had appeared remorseful, because Benjamin was now worthy of humanity?

How could he bear being near both of these women again? "I hardly think returning tomorrow will be necessary."

"Oh, please? I would be so grateful." Mrs. Bird rested a hand on his arm, lowering her voice. "Lucy is so very dear to me. I fear Dr. Chelton would have already tried to bleed her, foolish man, as he'd once tried to do with me. I'd never forgive myself if anything happened to her, you understand."

Benjamin drew a deep, calming breath, creating more room in his mind for his logic to return. It had been absent for far too long that morning.

"I would be happy to return tomorrow, Mrs. Bird." And he would be more than happy to use Mrs. Bird's money to fund Father's apothecary shop. "Until then, I suggest you offer Miss Lincoln a bit of warm broth then allow her the chance to rest. Her headache will likely worsen before it improves."

"Of course, Dr. Kent. I will see to her every need. And thank you so much for your help. We are indebted to you."

He gave a polite smile then swiftly shrugged away from her fingers still resting on his arm. She had to be nearly ten years his senior, but he didn't like women of any age attempting to flatter a man with their coquetry. Not after Miss Lincoln had done the very same to him.

Nettled, he scribbled down a prescription then tore it off and handed it to Mrs. Bird. She, in turn, scurried toward the lady's maid.

The women spoke together in hushed tones near the door as Benjamin replaced his booklet and pencil within the medical bag, careful to keep his eyes away from Miss Lincoln.

"Dr. Kent?"

Her soft voice cooed up at him, and he could do little else but meet her gaze. "Yes, Miss Lincoln?"

He was quite proud of the apathy in his tone.

"I wanted to thank you for helping me, even after…"

She trailed off, wincing. Was this a sign of her regret? But then, how much could she have changed—really?

He barricaded the iron bars around his heart, pushing away the logic he'd gathered before. He should be the adult, the better person. And yet…

"Even after what, Miss Lincoln?"

She paused. "After…after our last meeting."

She glanced to her aunt, who was still very much occupied with the lady's maid. The servant's eyes had grown significantly wider as she clearly attempted to remember all of Mrs. Bird's instructions.

Miss Lincoln lowered her voice even further. "After I declined your proposal."

The words shot a bolt of lightning through his core, singeing his insides and burning past the barrier round his heart with white-hot pain.

He'd been wrong this entire time. He hadn't overcome the hurt

24

from all those years ago. And hearing the words aloud only added to his embarrassment.

He snapped his bag shut with a swift clap, turning to face her with a deadened expression. "Declined? What need is there to dip your words into the sweetness of honey, when not even that can mask their bitterness?" He leaned closer to her, his jaw tight. "You *rejected* me, Miss Lincoln. You berated my proposal. You laughed at me in front of my parents and your friends."

She leaned back in her pillow, her brown eyes he'd once admired now brimming with tears. Tears, he was certain, caused by being reprimanded, not out of true regret.

But he did not stop, his words gaining power as he continued. "You told me that you could never marry me because I would stifle you. Because I would destroy who you were as a person. Based on the evidence, I could hardly believe you merely *declined* my proposal."

She sniffed. "But surely...surely enough time has passed for the two of us to move on. To even become fri—"

He held up his forefinger, silencing her ridiculous words. "I will return tomorrow and every day after that for as long as your aunt desires because that is my duty. But do not think for one moment I do such things out of friendship. That ship set sail years ago, Miss Lincoln, and I never wish to see its return. As you said before, we are far better without each other in our lives."

Her lip trembled, and she closed her eyes with a hand to her brow. Her head must be pulsing, thanks to Benjamin.

But he would not regret stating facts—stating the truth. Standing to his full height, he straightened his jacket and retrieved his bag. "Until tomorrow, Miss Lincoln."

With a single nod, he turned on his heel and left the room, waiting for the satisfaction to fill his soul after finally standing up to the girl who'd broken his heart and spirit so many years ago.

But the satisfaction never came.

# CHAPTER 4

*L*ucy thrummed her fingers against her covers, staring up at her gold-threaded bed hangings for what had to be the third hour straight. When Aunt Harriet had been at Lucy's bedside reading to her, the time had flown by. When Lucy had allowed sleep to grip her consciousness, that was even better.

But now, wide awake and alone, she could do nothing beyond lying down, for fear of aggravating her headache. If only she hadn't been so reckless at the Frost Fair. She should be talking over the final dinner plans with Aunt Harriet for Christmas tomorrow. She should be begging Aunt to purchase evergreen branches and holly berries, as per their usual tradition in Fawsley, Northamptonshire. Aunt was hardly bothered by such decorations, but Lucy was.

Still, she would look past the house being entirely un-festive if she could but leave her room for only a moment or two. Otherwise, how could she manage to obey Dr. Kent's orders and remain abed for another full day?

*Dr. Kent.* Her brow furrowed, the tightness in her neck feeding the pulsing at the back of her head. How strange it was to see him again. And how horribly discomfiting. She'd hardly recognized him, what with how comfortably he spoke with Aunt—and how blunt he'd been with Lucy.

He'd always been soft-spoken, seemingly afraid to say a word to anyone. Apart from his rather combative nature the morning before, the only time she'd ever known Dr. Kent to be straightforward was, well, when he'd proposed to her.

The thumping in her head increased, as if a spoon knocked against her skull over and over again. She'd deserved every word of censure the gentleman had tossed at her. She *had* been cruel four years ago. She'd been heartless. She deserved to be berated for her actions—just as much as he deserved an apology for them.

After he'd left yesterday, she'd tried to hide her tears beneath her hands, but Aunt Harriet was at her bedside in a single moment.

"It is merely the ache in my head, Aunt. That is all," Lucy had said.

"I've sent Wright to the apothecary's for the items we don't have. The worst will be over soon."

But Lucy had no hope that it would. Unless, of course, Dr. Kent had prescribed her with some draught that erased regret and sorrow for a past life.

A click at the door finally drew her attention away from her misery.

Aunt peeked her head into the room. "Did I wake you?"

"No, I've been awake for hours. Rather bored, as I'm sure you can imagine."

Aunt came fully into the room, closing the door behind her. She held a small, red box tied at the top with a brown string. "How are you feeling?"

"Perfectly well." Lucy plastered on her widest grin. "Even better than before, I daresay. Perhaps we ought to venture back to the Frost Fair. Or the bookshop you spoke of yesterday. Ever since you mentioned it, I've not been able to stop my thoughts from straying in that direction."

"The bookshop?" Her aunt's cheeks pinked. Was she...blushing? Since when did Aunt Harriet blush? "As much as I'd like to go there—

for you, of course—I believe it will be better if you stay in bed, my dear."

Lucy folded her arms, staring once more at her bed hangings.

"I know you dislike staying down even more than I do, Lucy, but if Dr. Kent insists, then I must, as well."

Lucy distractedly eyed the box still in Aunt's hands. "You've never listened to any physician or surgeon before now. Why is Dr. Kent any different?"

Aunt Harriet sat down on the chair beside Lucy's bed. "Because as dull as Dr. Kent appears to be, he did not bleed you for no apparent reason as Dr. Chelton would've been sure to do. I assure you, the moment Dr. Kent suggests such a remedy, he shall be shown the door and never allowed back."

Lucy smiled. Aunt Harriet didn't approve of most physicians, and Dr. Chelton was first and foremost. She'd developed her mistrust of doctors when Uncle Francis had passed. Since then, Aunt had taken it upon herself to have her own fully-stocked medicine chest and only relied on physicians when absolutely necessary.

Still, Lucy knew the real reason Dr. Kent had been written in Aunt's pretended book of good graces. It was because Aunt Harriet didn't really *know* who Dr. Kent was.

"We were friends in Fawsley," Lucy had explained the night before. "You've met him a number of times yourself, Aunt."

"Oh, no, that cannot be true. I'm certain I would've remembered such a handsome face."

Lucy had clamped her mouth shut then, avoiding any mention that Dr. Kent—the son of an apothecary—had proposed to her.

Aunt Harriet had never looked kindly at the working class, gentleman or not. That was precisely the reason Lucy had kept his past a forgotten memory for her guardian.

Lucy, like her parents, didn't refuse to associate with people simply because of their class. But Aunt would've surely snubbed Dr. Kent without a second thought, pushing him out of her house and Grosvenor Square altogether. Lucy could not allow poor Benjamin

Kent to be subjected to any more humiliation or rejection at her own hand or her aunt's.

That was the only reason she'd kept their past a secret. Not because there was something different about Dr. Kent that intrigued her—something she couldn't quite put her finger on. She hardly cared.

"Have you an objection to using Dr. Kent?"

Blinking, Lucy emerged from her thoughts to answer Aunt Harriet's question. "Objection? Not to him, per se. Only if he forces me to stay in bed any longer."

In truth, she very much wished for aunt to hire another physician, but that would only raise questions as to why and whom else she would hire. It was far easier to simply bear the discomfort of having Benjamin Kent examine her.

"You know I've always encouraged you to do what you wish, Lucy," Aunt said. "But in this one instance, I believe Dr. Kent is right. Rest will do wonders for you." She broke off with a shake of her head. "Heavens, I'm beginning to sound just like your mother and father, encouraging obedience from you."

A spark of light lit within Lucy. Would her parents arrive before Twelfth Night? "Have we received word from my parents yet?"

"I'm afraid not. No doubt your father chose to stay behind until the weather cleared." Aunt sighed. "Your mama would have taken the carriage and ridden straight through the fog when she was younger. But alas. People change, do they not?"

Lucy hid her frown. When her logic fled, Mama's soft encouragement prevailed, like when she'd prevented Lucy from swimming across an entire lake or walking atop a fence post. Lucy was more than happy to have the mother she did, even if Mama was more wary of certain things.

Aunt almost seemed to begrudge such logic. Was that because Mama had changed from carefree to careful? Or was Aunt more upset about *what* had changed Mama?

"I know what to do to make up for all my logical thinking," Aunt said, interrupting Lucy's thoughts again. Her eyes twinkled as she finally handed over the box.

"Aunt, you shouldn't have."

"I didn't. Mr. Carter stopped by earlier this morning to call on you. When I told him what had occurred, he left, only to return soon after with this."

Lucy tipped her head to the side, sighing at her friend's generosity. "I wish you would've told me he called. I would've gone down to meet him."

"That's precisely why I kept his presence unknown. I knew you could not help yourself. At any rate, I promised I would see that this was delivered to you. What is more exciting, however, is that when he first called, I invited him to dinner tomorrow evening, which he happily accepted."

Christmas with Aunt alone would have been delightful enough, but adding Mr. Carter would make the evening all the brighter. "Wonderful! Then we shall not have so small a Christmas dinner as we feared."

"This is all dependent on if Dr. Kent deems you well enough to come down, of course." Aunt stood from her chair. "So you'd better rest now, I think."

Lucy's improved mood vanished in an instant. Thank heavens Dr. Kent had never been a vindictive sort. She'd fear he'd make her suffer in her room for longer just to retaliate after what she'd done to him.

Aunt placed a kiss to her brow. "I've a few callers this afternoon, so I will come to see you after they depart and give you a full report of their visit. Until then, I'll leave orders that you are not to be disturbed so you may receive a little sleep."

"Thank you, Aunt."

After another kiss, Aunt Harriet departed, and Lucy was left alone with her box from Mr. Carter. With careful movements, she shifted against her mattress, propping herself up on multiple pillows until she was comfortable.

Her head spun from the exertion, so she secured both hands on the bed. Once her vision straightened, she reached for the box beside her.

Before the lid had fully been removed, the spicy-sweet aroma tickled her nose. She knew exactly what Mr. Carter had brought for her.

"Mince pies."

She grinned, eagerly eying the small pastries, their golden tops lightly dusted with white sugar—like the first signs of snow atop an untraveled, country road.

Without hesitation, she dug into the box and took her first bite of the delectable dessert, sighing with pleasure.

Aunt would no doubt say Mr. Carter was hinting at some burgeoning feelings for Lucy what with such a gift, but Lucy knew her friend better than that.

When their families would join for meals during Christmastide, Mr. Carter and Lucy would often quarrel over the mince pies. She'd caught him more than once sneaking them into his pockets for later, thereby preventing her from having as many as she wished—not to mention creating quite the mess for his servants to clean up later.

Mr. Carter was clearly attempting to make amends for his childish behavior, not implying some abiding love for Lucy.

She sank her teeth into yet another bite, flavor seeping across her tongue in delightful punches. She could eat these all day.

Going in for another mouthful, however, her eyes caught onto a small slip of paper at the bottom of the box. She shuffled the sweets aside and pulled out the closed letter, unfolding it to discover Mr. Carter's slanted handwriting.

Sly boy, hiding the letter beneath the pies. Had Aunt been aware of his correspondence, she would have certainly assumed a relationship between them. Again.

Nibbling at another pie, she combed through the words carefully, the back-and-forth movement causing her eyes to smart.

*Miss Lincoln,*

*How saddened I was to hear news of your accident. Of course, I'm not at all surprised that you were injured due to chasing after a pastry. I know your love of mince pies better than I know your dislike for remaining indoors.*

*Speaking of such, why are you still abed? I wonder how your aunt has managed such a feat. Has she been threatening you? Of course, I jest. But perhaps you ought to prove your stamina to her, simply show her you are well. I'm sure your proud nature can concoct an event to reveal just that.*

*I do hope you are well before Christmas, especially now that we are to dine together. I've such exciting news to share with you, news that I only was able to hint at the day before. I've met a woman. And not just any woman—one who might convince me to settle down, marry, and start a family. She enjoys mince pies as greatly as you do and brightens every room she enters. I tell you such things in the strictest of confidence, of course. Should my mother discover I'm apt to finally wed, well, I might just attempt to prove her wrong once again.*

*I will tell you more tomorrow—when you are healthy and well and have come down for a hearty dinner.*

*Your friend,*
*Mr. Carter*

Lucy set down the letter, still shaking her head in surprise at his revelation. So her suspicions had been accurate. Mr. Carter had found a woman to marry. That would certainly be just the thing to convince Aunt Harriet that he was not the gentleman for Lucy.

Thank heavens.

Finally setting the box down, she carefully leaned the side of her head against the mahogany headboard. A moment ticked by. Then another.

She stared at the bare trees outside that trembled in the frigid, winter wind. Then she eyed the book on her bedside table Aunt had read to her that morning.

She really ought to sleep. But her mind refused to rest or settle on anything but Mr. Carter's suggestion.

*But perhaps you ought to prove your stamina to her, simply show her you are well.*

Lucy chewed her lip, anxiously wiggling her toes beneath her covers. She'd never disobeyed her aunt's express desires before. Her parents would wish for Lucy to remain abed, as well. They would never risk her health. If she chose to leave, she'd be outright betraying them all.

Or would she be proving that she was in control of her own health and could do as she wished—just as Aunt had always done?

With a determined set to her jaw, Lucy flung back her covers and bounded up from the bed.

# CHAPTER 5

*U*nfortunately, Lucy's swift movements caused her head to spin and pulled her right back down to her covers.

"Slower, Lucy," she warned herself.

Rising much more gingerly, she stood again, moving step by step until her eyes no longer jittered back and forth. The fact that she was dizzy clearly meant that she'd spent far too long in bed. Nothing else.

In silence, she worked to replace her dressing gown with a dress, taking three times longer than usual without the help of her lady's maid. Martha was certainly trustworthy, but Lucy would hate to embroil her maid in Lucy's subterfuge and force her to keep secrets.

Thank heavens her pelisse would cover the buttons she couldn't do up. And thank heavens her bonnet would cover her disheveled, bird's-nest hair. She had to pin the natural curls a bit higher than usual, due to her still-pulsing wound, but that hardly mattered. She wouldn't be removing her bonnet anyway, nor was she planning on even speaking with anyone.

She just wanted to go out of doors for a brief moment to breathe in the fresh air—and to prove that she knew her wellness better than Dr. Kent, or any physician for that matter.

She took a quick glance into the mirror, twirling a few curls near her temples, then tucked in the rest. That would do well enough.

Knowing the servants had been tasked to keep away from her chambers—and that Aunt would be occupied in the parlor with her guests—Lucy wasn't terribly frightened of being discovered.

As such, she abruptly skittered her way down the stairs and through the corridors, bracing herself against the bannister and walls to keep from falling flat on her face due to her whirling head.

Finally, she reached the entryway, and she noiselessly slipped out of doors, securing the door behind her.

Another wave of dizziness brushed over her, but a blast of frosty air cloaked her face and lungs, causing her to momentarily and bliss-fully forget the fresh ache in her head.

She grinned. There. If she was so unwell, could she have gotten dressed alone and left the townhome without aid? She thought not.

In fact, she was feeling so healthy, she had a mind to jaunt farther into Town. She still needed to purchase that gift for Papa, especially if he and Mama made it to London before Twelfth Night. He always gave Lucy the most thoughtful of gifts—drawing pencils, strands of pearls, a new fur muff. She would be remiss if she did not get him a gift this year. Never mind that she was unchaperoned. Aunt would surely understand Lucy's reasoning.

With decided steps, she marched down the outer stairs of the townhome, only to stop at the bottom with a wince and a gentle hand to the back of her bonnet.

The thick snow blanketing the pathway glared brightly against her vision. She closed her eyes, reaching out a few times before her gloved hand clasped the frosted, iron railing nearby.

The pain would pass. It always did. And yet, each moment she stood, the blood seemed to pulse harder and harder against her wound, as if catching up from her jaunting.

Perhaps returning indoors would be for the best. Lucy could clearly make it farther into Town if she really wished to, but...she didn't have her maid with her, nor did she want to disappoint her aunt. At any rate, she didn't have her reticule or coins either, and Father was sure to be more pleased with his daughter's health than any gift she might give him.

Yes, returning inside would be best.

She turned around, her eyes still closed as she planted her boot on the first step of the townhome.

"Miss Lincoln?"

Lucy gasped, opening her eyes and spinning toward the voice that called her name. "Dr. Kent?"

She didn't know why she was surprised. Short of being discovered by Aunt Harriet, Dr. Kent would be the obvious choice with which fate should choose to embarrass her.

He stood beside a tall, dark-haired woman, whom Lucy recognized as Miss Parfitt, a young lady she'd met last Season at a ball in Town. The pretty creature—whose maid stood silently and obediently behind her—looked rather pleased to be on the arm of Dr. Kent.

Lucy struggled to keep her eyes from popping. She'd never seen Benjamin Kent with a woman before. Not one so close to him, at any rate. Were the two of them...

"Might I ask what you are doing out of doors?"

Lucy's attention swiveled back to Dr. Kent. Wiping the wince from her eyes, she delivered her most pleasant expression. "Why, I'm simply getting a touch of fresh air." She turned back to the woman on his arm, somehow delivering a curtsy without falling over. "Lovely to see you again, Miss Parfitt."

Miss Parfitt nodded with her signature friendly smile. "And you, Miss Lincoln."

Her rosy cheeks and shining curls made Lucy acutely aware of her own unkempt state—tangled locks and no doubt gaunt skin. But she hardly need impress this woman *or* this gentleman.

"I believe my instructions were for you to remain abed for the next day or two." Dr. Kent's words cut through the silence once again. He was apparently unaware of anything else occurring apart from Lucy's dereliction.

Thoughts of their last meeting flickered in her mind, and she shifted her feet. She needed to apologize for what had happened between them four years ago, for her cruelty, but she could hardly do such a thing in front of Miss Parfitt—or now that she'd been caught red-handed in her betrayal of both his and her aunt's advisement.

"Yes, those were your instructions, Dr. Kent," she returned with nonchalance. "And I assure you, I have every intention to adhere them. Just as soon as I finish my stroll."

He eyed her unmoving skirts then faced Miss Parfitt. "Would you mind very much if you went along without me for a moment? I must discuss something of importance with my patient."

Miss Parfitt nodded at once. "Of course, Dr. Kent."

He gave her a charming half-smile Lucy hadn't known he possessed, leaning closer to Miss Parfitt with a whisper. "I won't be long."

Miss Parfitt slipped her arm from his, and with a lingering smile of her own in his direction, and a departing curtsy for Lucy, she continued down the road with her lady's maid at her heels.

Lucy stared after the feminine swish of her skirts, catching Dr. Kent doing the same. There was certainly something between that woman and the physician. The Dr. Kent Lucy knew had been hardly able to look at a woman, let alone flirt. The most he'd ever done with Lucy was ask her to dance before he'd proposed, and even then he'd avoided eye contact.

Well, people changed, she supposed, just like Aunt had said. And if he was to marry Miss Parfitt, Lucy was more than happy for him.

"Does your aunt know you are out of doors, Miss Lincoln?"

Dr. Kent's eyes fell on her, the charm he'd displayed before dissipating as swiftly as Lucy's will to remain standing. She leaned more heavily on the iron railing, turning to face him.

"You truly believe I could dress alone and sneak outside of Aunt's townhome without her notice? Really, Dr. Kent, you give me too much credit."

That wasn't exactly lying now, was it?

Dr. Kent didn't respond, his green eyes peering down at her without any indication as to what he could be thinking.

He'd done the very same when they were younger. Growing up, no one had ever known what Benjamin Kent was thinking. His responses were only ever one or two words, apart from when he'd proposed to Lucy—commanding a total of *four* words instead.

Mr. Carter had always teased that there was nothing in Dr. Kent's head, that he stared mutely because he had no notion of what to say. But Lucy had always known better than to believe that. Dr. Kent was far too intelligent to have nothing in his mind. She believed instead that he was merely observing others in order to understand them better—just like he was doing right now.

And right now, it felt as if he was reading her very thoughts.

And if that was true, then he knew she was lying.

Her gloved fingers wiggled against her skirts, and stress crept up the back of her neck, wrapping its tight fingers around her already pulsing head.

The rambling…it was coming. No matter the relaxing techniques she practiced—breathing deeply, placing her thoughts elsewhere, encouraging herself to have peace—nothing helped.

There was no use. The words gurgled inside her like a steaming pot of white soup, boiling over the edge and spilling all around her.

"Good heavens, Dr. Kent. How you stare so. I merely came out of doors to stretch my legs. My aunt, well, she may not know the entire truth about my being out here, but she certainly would hold no objection if I was well, and you can clearly see that I *am* well. I would not be standing here if I wasn't more than capable of doing so. I merely hold onto this railing because it cools me down, as I'm unbearably overheated at the moment. Not that I feel feverish, of course. I'm a perfect temperature, I assure you. My cheeks are merely reddened due to the cool air now, which, I can positively say, is marvelous and helping me more than remaining indoors would, as I…I…"

What was happening? Was she stopping? Her words had never before ceased on their own. Once her nervous rambling began, she would continue until someone stopped her—usually Aunt, who couldn't abide the embarrassment of the terrible trait.

But Dr. Kent hadn't said a word. He'd smiled.

When she used to flirt with him—mentioning the lovely green of his eyes or declaring him to be the smartest gentleman in all of Northamptonshire—he'd always averted his gaze and hid his smile behind a deepening blush. Unfortunately, this had only proven to boost Lucy's ego.

But now, his shining eyes and wide grin captured her. For all she could remember, this was the first time she'd seen his genuine, full smile. It was mesmerizing. Mesmerizing and unnerving.

"What is so amusing to you, Dr. Kent?"

Benjamin had never had the upper hand when it came to Lucy Lincoln. With a single glance from her, he used to crumble apart like an overcooked Christmas pudding and turn as red as the holly berries on top.

That wasn't to say Miss Lincoln didn't get embarrassed. He distinctly remembered each time she'd rambled when she was in the midst of large crowds of strangers or before fine lords and ladies. But until this point, she'd never revealed any anxiousness around Benjamin. Excepting, of course, when he stared at her.

That told him two things: she had just been caught in a lie, and she knew that *he* knew.

Such a fact caused his smile and confidence to grow tenfold.

"Do you know I am acquainted well enough with your aunt to know how alike the two of you are, Miss Lincoln?"

She hesitated. "I suppose."

"I know the both of you to be headstrong, impulsive, independent. And extremely stubborn."

Her lips pulled down at his very accurate description of the both of them.

He continued. "However, I do believe that as headstrong as Mrs.

Bird is, no matter how she pushes you to be as independent as possible, there is not a chance on this frozen earth that she would have agreed to you coming out of doors. She cares for you too greatly to even consider putting you in further danger."

"Perhaps, but I—"

"There is no point in refuting my claim, Miss Lincoln. I know the truth."

Her lips clamped in a pout.

"Now," he said, securing his gloves, "you had better return indoors, or I will be forced to report your delinquency to her."

She scoffed. Her own black gloves still grasped the frosty railing, and she leaned closer to it. The front of her bodice bunched up oddly, as if her dress wasn't done-up properly at the back.

What was he doing, noting such a thing? He blinked, drawing his attention back to her narrowed eyes.

"You wouldn't dare tell my aunt," she said.

He raised his brows boldly. "Wouldn't I?"

He could see her inner struggle play out in the ever-increasing frown—should she believe Benjamin, or should she take a risk and stay out of doors for longer?

He didn't regret confronting Miss Lincoln about their past the day before, but he *did* regret losing control of his temper and his logic. So now, having command of not only his own reactions but also of their conversation, composure infused his entire being.

"Listen here, Dr. Kent," she finally responded, "you really are creating something out of nothing. Threatening to inform my aunt that I am merely taking a stroll out of doors is simply preposterous. Have you nothing better to do?"

"On the contrary, Miss Lincoln. As your physician, I am quite aware of your injury, as well as what might occur if you do not take care. I must insist you return indoors immediately."

She waved a dismissive hand. "I am perfectly well."

"You cannot even stand on your own."

"I can." She removed her hand, standing still for a moment, staring straight ahead before she teetered forward with wide eyes and a quick yelp.

Before she could fall into the snow, Benjamin lunged forward, catching her in his arms. The scent of mince pies sailed under his nose as her slight body fell against him. His heart tripped—but only due to his fear of having one of his patients nearly injure herself again.

"Do you see, Miss Lincoln? What *perfectly well* person cannot stand on her own two feet?"

She leaned her head back, still grasping the lapels of his jacket to keep steady. "Perhaps you…"

Her words trailed off when she found his eyes. They stood in silence, her gaze trailing over his features deliberately, thoroughly, before settling on his mouth. She tipped her head to the side with curiosity, as if trying to comprehend what she was looking at.

Benjamin forced his breathing to remain steady, struggling to keep from examining her so comprehensively, as well. He couldn't help but take in her disheveled curls, her rosy cheeks, her brown eyes still bright, despite wincing from her headache.

There was a time when being this close to her—when having her eyes on him in such an intimate way—would have sent his heart racing wildly. How long had he dreamt of this proximity, of holding her so closely to him?

But that dream had faded away many years ago. And he'd had enough of her scrutinizing.

Grasping her upper arms, he carefully helped her to stand away from him. "I will help you to the door. Will you be able to manage the rest of the way to your bedchamber?"

Her eyes lingered on him. "You won't be taking me the entire way?"

He didn't have time to do such a thing. He needed to meet with Miss Parfitt.

Blast. He'd nearly forgotten about the woman. She would have no doubt made it to the teashop already. Her parents would be arriving shortly, too. He needed to leave now before they'd finished with the warm refreshment and he froze for longer in front of Miss Lincoln's home.

"My presence will only bring more awareness to your having gone out of doors." He offered Miss Lincoln his arm, and she accepted it, leaning heavily against him as they took their first step. "I shan't tell your aunt what has occurred, either, so long as you promise to practice good sense where your health is concerned from this point forward."

Her pride was nettled, as was evident by the slight lowering of her brows, but she nodded all the same. "I appreciate your discretion."

They completed their ascent, and Miss Lincoln removed her arm from his to use the door as her support instead.

He really ought to offer his help the rest of the way, but then, Miss Lincoln had gotten herself into this predicament. She should be the one to get herself out of it.

But blast his conscience. "If you require aid, I would be more than happy to assist you the rest of the way."

"No, that is quite all right." She tucked a stray curl farther into her bonnet. "Thank you, though. And thank you for yesterday. After what I did to you, I hardly expected you to…You are a fine gentleman, sir."

Perhaps had his heart not been surrounded by a layer of ice thicker than what was now atop the River Thames, he would have accepted her gratitude for what it was—a simple compliment.

But his heart was impenetrable. "It is unfortunate I was not so fine a gentleman before I became more than the apothecary's son, is it not?"

She pulled back, shaking her head as a thin crease formed down the center of her eyebrows.

Before she could say a word, Benjamin delivered a tight smile. He didn't need to hear her weak attempt to refute his claim. "I will return this evening for my scheduled visit. Good day, Miss Lincoln."

He tipped his hat then trotted down the stairs without a glance back. Miss Lincoln would be more than fine returning to her bedchambers alone. She was stubborn enough to do so without any help at all.

Thank heavens Miss Parfitt wasn't stubborn. Not that he knew the young woman well, of course. He'd only met her a time or two in the last month. But he was determined to get to know her better that morning—and to enjoy a steaming cup of tea and even perhaps some gingerbread.

Although, now that he thought about it, a mince pie might satisfy him more than gingerbread at this point.

But where such a craving had come from, he had no idea.

No idea at all.

# CHAPTER 6

*L*ucy lay wide awake in bed that night, thoughts swarming like honeybees to the last asters of autumn. She had overdone it that day, as frustrating as it was to admit.

She needed to be diligent in resting tomorrow if she was going to be well enough to join Aunt Harriet and Mr. Carter for Christmas dinner.

Although, if Dr. Kent was to be believed, she'd have no problem being well enough to go downstairs for the meal.

What a day she'd shared with that man. From being discovered sneaking away from home to being examined for a second time, she was quite ready to be finished with him.

After creeping back into her chambers without notice, Lucy had barely managed to undress before falling soundly asleep until well after dinner.

Despite a little grogginess from so much rest, Lucy's head no longer spun, and the ache from her wound had lessened to a bearable dull—for which she was eternally grateful.

"You are looking particularly robust this evening, Miss Lincoln," Dr. Kent had said when he'd arrived, checking her pulse in her wrist.

"If I didn't know any better, I'd say your rosy cheeks were due to receiving a bit of fresh air."

Heat had crept up her neck, and she'd prayed Aunt Harriet wouldn't notice. Dr. Kent had promised discretion. If Lucy hadn't known any better, she would've said the man had actually been *teasing* her. But the Dr. Kent she knew had never teased a soul in his life.

"Fortunately, Mrs. Bird," Dr. Kent had continued as he'd felt the bump on Lucy's head, "your niece has more sense than to go out of doors."

"Yes, she may take after my headstrong behavior, but she'd never be *that* reckless," Aunt had agreed.

Lucy twisted to her side in bed, lying her cheek against her open palm. After Aunt's comment, Dr. Kent had flashed his eyes knowingly in Lucy's direction, and she'd struggled to keep her smile at bay.

Perhaps he *had* been teasing. He could've been, what with the way he'd changed in every other regard. Even his physical appearance had altered some.

When she'd fallen into him earlier that day, she'd taken the opportunity to peruse his face for the first time since they'd been reunited. She wasn't surprised to see he was still as handsome as ever—his green eyes just as bright, his jawline just as angled.

But his face had slimmed, and his cheekbones were more prominent than before. And there was something else. His stance, his confidence. He was more self-assured than he ever was. That was what had captured her attention. That was why she'd been unable to pry her eyes away from him.

And that was no doubt why Miss Parfitt had been walking with him.

Lucy sighed, shifting against her mattress to lie on her back. She propped her hands at the base of her head to avoid her bruise pressing against the pillow.

Was Benjamin Kent truly attached to Miss Parfitt? The woman was beautiful and elegant, if not a little soft-spoken. But then, that was exactly the sort of person who would fit well with Dr. Kent, wasn't it?

At any rate, what business was this of hers?

She placed a hand over her eyes. She'd felt odd all day long, disappointed and empty inside, like she'd misplaced her favorite parasol. It had been that way ever since…ever since seeing Dr. Kent looking at Miss Parfitt. It had been exactly the way he'd once looked at Lucy—with admiration. Now he merely regarded her with indifference.

She knew she shouldn't care. After all, she didn't love him any more than he still loved her. But she'd never had to share in his attention before. At balls, dinner parties, or even walking through town, his eyes had always remained on her.

She ought to be glad someone else had caught his fancy. Someone so beautiful and regal. Someone who didn't appear outside half-buttoned with disheveled hair and mince pie on her breath.

With an impatient groan, she rolled onto her other side, staring out her window at the softly falling snow. She was quite finished appearing in shambles each time she saw the gentleman. First, she'd fallen on her backside at the Frost Fair, then she'd turned into a weeping mess when she'd attempted to apologize for wronging him. That morning, she'd nearly died of humiliation after being caught lying to and disobeying her aunt.

No, she did not love Dr. Kent, but that didn't mean she didn't want to appear her best in front of him.

She rubbed her eyes now dry from lack of sleep. Tomorrow was Christmas, and it would be the last time she saw Dr. Kent. There really was no reason for her to see him again once she was well.

So she would dress her best. Not for him, mind. Merely for her own self-preservation. And if he just so happened to look at her with that same admiration he had four years ago, that was fine with her.

The next morning, Lucy awoke without a headache. She stretched her arms high overhead with a contented sigh as her eyes wandered to the window. Snow still fell softly outside, a fresh fire crackled warmly in the hearth, and the sweet smell of piping hot chocolate tickled her nose.

What a glorious start to what was sure to be an even more glorious Christmas day.

Aunt Harriet had requested for Lucy not to strain herself by attending church that day, so Lucy remained in bed, nibbling on a few biscuits and sipping her chocolate.

She would miss the sermon that morning—listening to the story of the Christ child and singing hymns that glorified His birth—but Lucy was determined not to set back the progress she'd finally made, ridding herself of that blasted headache. And she wouldn't do anything to upset the possibility of joining Aunt Harriet and Mr. Carter for Christmas dinner that evening.

Beyond Mr. Carter's cryptic note the day before, Lucy had received no further knowledge about the woman he'd supposedly fallen for, and she was anxious to learn more about who had captured her friend's heart.

Unfortunately, Lucy's fate still rested in the hands of Dr. Kent. Aunt was determined to keep Lucy upstairs until the physician deemed it safe to leave her chambers. *Fortunately*, Lucy was well enough to leave her room this time—and she knew her plan to prove her health would succeed.

An hour later, Aunt Harriet returned with a full report of the services, sharing the well wishes the congregation had for Lucy before asking how her niece was feeling.

"Better than ever, Aunt," Lucy responded truthfully.

Aunt Harriet beamed. "I'm so glad to hear it. I've a surprise for you downstairs, providing Dr. Kent agrees to your removal from your chambers."

"How thoughtful of you," Lucy said. "I should add that we ought not be too concerned over what the physician will say. I'm certain he will be more than pleased with my progress."

And hopefully her appearance.

Not expecting Dr. Kent until just before dinner, Lucy and Aunt Harriet spent the rest of the day together in Lucy's room, reading books, singing Christmas carols, and playing cribbage, piquet, and speculation—all while snacking on mince pies, gingerbread biscuits, and Shrewsbury cakes.

When the sun's light no longer cast golden shadows through the window, and London was awash in a cool, navy blue, the two of them parted to make ready for the evening.

"What do we have planned for your hair, miss?" Martha asked when she joined Lucy in her room. "The usual chignon?"

"I was hoping for something a little more...memorable."

Martha smiled. "I know just the thing, miss."

As her lady's maid carefully worked around the bump still tender at the back of Lucy's head, Lucy's thoughts wandered to her family. She still had hope for their arrival by Twelfth Night, good weather permitting, but she would miss them tonight. Christmas evening with her parents had always held a special place in her heart.

They often enjoyed a quiet dinner at home, then she would accompany her father's singing before they ended the evening with a chapter from the latest book they were reading together, all while Mama listened with a happy smile. It was simple, but those moments had always been her most poignant of every Christmastide.

"Will that suffice, miss?" Martha asked, drawing Lucy's attention back to the present as the lady's maid set aside the curling tongs and propped her hands on her hips.

Lucy moved her head back and forth in the mirror. With the added work of her bruise, her gathered mass of curls had to be raised slightly higher towards the top of her head, but this only proved to heighten her long neck. Deep red holly berries and strands of white pearls adorned her locks, while blonde ringlets modestly decorated her temples.

"You've outdone yourself, Martha. Truly, I love it."

"I'm pleased, miss. Shall I help you dress now?"

In a matter of moments, Lucy had donned her deep red gown tied with a white ribbon around the bodice, secured a strand of pearls around her neck, and finished off the look with a touch of rouge to her lips and cheeks.

"Perfect, miss," Martha said, admiring her handiwork. "I hope you have the happiest of Christmases."

Lucy reached forward, embracing the maid who'd been with her for more than six years. "I wish the same for you, Martha."

The door clicked open, and Aunt Harriet popped her head into the room. "Oh, Lucy. How beautiful you look."

Lucy beamed, smiling at Martha who stepped back with a humble smile. "As do you, Aunt."

Aunt Harriet peered down at her cream-colored gown. "It's not so very a festive color as yours is, but it will do for an old widow." She winked, reaching for Lucy's hands. "Am I safe to assume you have no intention of remaining in your room for dinner this evening?" She raised a knowing brow. "I suppose it is just as well. I don't think I'd wish for you to stay here, either. However, I would like to know Dr. Kent's opinion still. Come, he will arrive soon. We shall meet with him in my dressing room."

Lucy's stomach tumbled. Why was she so nervous? This was merely an opportunity to redeem herself, to prove she was not always in disarray around the gentleman. To prove that she was more than well enough to dine with Aunt Harriet this Christmas.

What this certainly was *not* was proving to herself and Dr. Kent that she was just as lovely as Miss Parfitt. She hardly cared how she measured up to the woman.

Reaching Aunt's dressing room, Lucy took a seat on one of the floral-cushioned chairs nearest the fire, leaning back against the curved, white wood. The curtains were drawn, allowing a cool draft to sail about the room from the darkened winter air, but the warmth from the small hearth permeated around her stronger.

"Mr. Carter will certainly find you very pleasant to peer at this evening."

Lucy's warning gaze snapped to Aunt's. "I did not dress this way to impress my friend." Nor did she dress that way to impress a certain physician.

"I was merely stating a fact."

She smiled innocently, but Lucy read between the lines. She

opened her mouth to inform Aunt of Mr. Carter finding a woman he wished to marry, but the door opened, and a servant entered the dressing room.

It was just as well. She shouldn't reveal that Mr. Carter had sent a note to her anyway.

"Dr. Kent, ma'am," the servant announced, backing away from the door to allow the physician inside the room.

Lucy stood, heart hopping like a newborn filly as she clasped her white gloved hands before her.

Dr. Kent's pleasant smile reached Aunt first, but when he turned to Lucy, it faltered.

There it was, that elusive expression Lucy had longed to see. His eyes softened and lingered on her, his brow raising just a fraction with pleasure. The glance lasted only a moment, but the admiration was clear—familiar. It was the same expression he'd had the night he'd proposed, when he'd been unable to keep from staring at her as they'd danced.

Instead of staring now, though, he cleared his throat and faced Aunt Harriet instead. "Mrs. Bird, Miss Lincoln. I wish you the compliments of the season this evening."

Despite his looking away so swiftly, Lucy bit her lip to keep from grinning. She needed to maintain humility, but there was something so satisfying knowing that a gentleman as handsome as he was *still* found her attractive.

"We are so grateful you agreed to come here on Christmas, sir." Aunt Harriet waved him farther into the room. "Please, do what you must so we do not keep you from your own celebrations this evening."

"Thank you, Mrs. Bird." Dr. Kent placed his bag on a small table near the fire. "I shall do my best to make haste."

He withdrew the same little booklet and pencil from his bag. "I must say, I wonder at you requiring my visit, Mrs. Bird, as it would appear that Miss Lincoln is determined to attend your dinner whether I advise it or not."

Aunt cheerfully laughed. "My Lucy will not be kept from what she desires, you know."

"Indeed." Dr. Kent returned her smile, shifting his back to Lucy.

"I did stay in my bed, though, just as you instructed, Dr. Kent." Lucy leaned slightly to the side, but he didn't meet her gaze. Why would he not look at her?

"Shall we begin, Miss Lincoln? I've just a few things to ask you, as per usual."

He rattled off his questions just like before, and she responded with ease, only unsettled by how he focused on his scribblings rather than on her.

Another knock sounded at the door, and Aunt stood from her seat across from Lucy. "Such a busy house today. Excuse me. I'll be just a moment."

She crossed the room, answering the door and speaking in hushed tones to Mrs. Jensen, the housekeeper, whose stern brow was wrinkled with worry.

There must be an issue with dinner. No doubt Aunt would see to it, and all would be well soon enough.

The soft scratching of pencil on paper drew Lucy's attention back to Dr. Kent, who still wrote in his book.

"What are you writing about so madly in there?" she asked, tipping her head to the side. "It must be very entertaining, indeed."

He continued writing. "Just a few notes."

Lucy stared up at his focused gaze. Perhaps he was simply anxious to leave for the Parfitts' home, to see Miss Parfitt again. That is where he would be dining, obviously, having no family of his own in Town.

At the thought of his leaving, Lucy's smile faltered. She and Martha had spent far too long on Lucy's hair and dress that evening for it only to be admired by this gentleman for a mere moment.

Perhaps she could prolong his visit, strike up a conversation so he might be coerced into remaining for longer and perhaps even venture a glance toward her.

"Have you more questions for me?" she asked.

He kept his head down. "In a moment."

Well, that hadn't worked. "Are you enjoying your Christmas Day?"

"Yes, thank you."

That hadn't either. "Mr. Martin Carter is dining with us this evening. Do you remember him from Fawsley?"

His jaw flinched, and he sent a quick glance toward her from the corner of his eye. "How could I forget?"

Ah, that had done it. Although, based on his lowered brow and frowning lips, this conversation might not be welcome. Dr. Kent and Mr. Carter had never exactly been friends, what with Mr. Carter's constant teasing of Dr. Kent's excessive reading and lack of speaking.

Surely Dr. Kent could not still begrudge the man for that.

"Have you had the opportunity to see Mr. Carter while living in London?" she asked next.

"I'm afraid I haven't. How does your head fare?"

Perhaps the man *did* hold a grudge. Why else would he change the subject so abruptly? "The ache is gone, though when I move swiftly, I feel a little dizzy."

"That is to be expected."

She narrowed her eyes. If she didn't know any better, she would have said Dr. Kent was frustrated, even annoyed with her attempt to engage him in conversation.

Well, she would try a different approach then. "Will you be dining with the Parfitts this evening?"

His gaze sailed toward her and remained. *Finally.* "Why would I be?"

"I just assumed, after seeing the two of you together."

"No, I will not be dining with them. Have you experienced any nausea since I last saw you?"

Well that conversation clearly had not worked, either. But she was not one to give up so easily. "No, I haven't felt unwell at all. If you are not dining with the Parfitts this evening, with whom *will* you be dining?"

The question was a bit presumptuous. He must have thought so, as well, for he closed his booklet shut with a short clap, placing it on the table and facing her. "I will be dining alone, Miss Lincoln. In the peace and solitude I so desire."

The smile slipped from her lips. Where was the teasing man from yesterday, the man who'd smiled so charmingly at Miss Parfitt?

Lucy hardly deserved his admiration anymore, but she'd tried so hard that evening.

"As I'm quite certain you are determined to dine with your aunt and...Mr. Carter this evening," Dr. Kent said, a slight pause before naming Mr. Carter, "I needn't conduct a full examination. I will, however, need to feel your pulse and your wound if you do not mind."

"No, please."

She straightened in her chair as he maneuvered around her, removing his gloves before his soft fingers weaved round her curls. The movement made a single, wispy strand of hair brush against her bare neck, but she warded off the pleasant shiver sliding up her spine just in time. She'd hate for him to think he'd elicited such a response from her due to his touch.

She glanced to the door, moving her head only a fraction. Aunt was still engaged in quiet conversation with the housekeeper, though Mrs. Jensen appeared far more at ease.

Lucy faced forward. "I must thank you again for keeping quiet about my escape yesterday, Dr. Kent," she whispered. "You will be pleased to know I have followed your orders and remained in bed since yesterday morning."

"Yes, so you've told me."

She frowned. His brief, no-nonsense words were far too similar to how he had spoken as a young man. She'd never been able to decipher what he was thinking or feeling.

With a soft sigh, she peered out the window. The snow had stopped for a moment, though the bare branches of the trees just outside the window were iced with glowing, white flakes.

"I'm so pleased to have snow this Christmas," she said. His fingers softly brushed against her tender bruise. "Although, I'm certain I would not enjoy it so greatly were I required to travel in it, like my poor parents."

No response.

"Do you recall those Christmases in Fawsley when the snow would be so deep, we could hardly make it to church?"

"Indeed."

She would get this man to smile, to become the same gentleman he'd been with Miss Parfitt, if it was the last thing she did. "We had many pleasant Christmases there, did we not? Always such lovely memories. The dinners we'd have with everyone in town, the nights filled with card games, and the Twelfth Night masquerades. Oh, and my favorite, the assembly that was always held on St. Stephen's Day."

She gasped, jerking up in her seat as his sudden increased pressure on her bruise sent shocks of pain through her head.

"My apologies," Dr. Kent mumbled.

He immediately withdrew his fingers from her locks and came around to sit on the chair before her. The pink on his cheeks told her his actions hadn't been on purpose.

She studied his once-familiar blush. "That is quite all right, of course. So long as you did not damage my curls."

He reached for his booklet and pencil. "No, I did not."

Was her teasing smile not obvious enough?

"May I?" He motioned to her wrist.

She offered him her arm, and he pressed his fingers atop her glove, eying the gold watch he'd pulled from his waistcoat.

With a stinted sigh, she stared off into the crackling fire. She'd tried everything with the man. Well, not everything, but she couldn't do *that*.

Slowly, her eyes traveled back to his. Perhaps...perhaps she could do exactly *that*. After all, it had always worked when they were younger as she'd attempted to draw him from his shell.

She really shouldn't stoop so low, but then, she was desperate. And just this once wouldn't hurt either of them, would it?

Wetting her lips, she leaned slightly forward, keeping her voice low and her conscience lower. "You know, Dr. Kent, I don't believe you've changed very much at all."

He hummed in response, still eying the watch. When he was

younger, he couldn't maintain her eye contact. Now it seemed as if he was willfully not looking at her.

"Oh, in some ways you certainly have," she continued. "But you are still just as contemplative as before. Still just as intelligent. Still just as...handsome."

His eyes flickered toward her, but he made no further reaction.

Lucy, however, cringed inwardly. Her guilt dripped from her heart and burned in her stomach. How could she have done this, even while knowing how she'd hurt him before? It had been years since she'd last flirted in such an obvious way.

But something was pulling her forward, an invisible force that would not rest until she received the attention she so desired from this man—no matter how much it sickened her.

She glanced to Aunt Harriet, who tapped distractedly on her chin as Mrs. Jensen whispered more words to her.

Their conversation was surely coming to an end. Lucy had to receive something from Dr. Kent—*anything*.

She focused her attention on him again. "I do wish you'd smile more, sir. I always loved your smile, though I hardly ever saw it fully."

His lips didn't flinch.

"I'm certain many a woman would enjoy the sight, too, if given the opportunity. You might even make a lady swoon."

She twittered a laugh, her stomach roiling at the sound.

How she despised herself. How she could not stop herself. How she couldn't understand what the devil it meant that—even now—she craved his attention.

His fingers pressed harder against her wrist in response to her giggle. Could he not feel her heartbeat enough through her glove? Or was he fighting off a smile? She had to be close to pulling it out now, hadn't she, so she could finally end this terrible charade?

"To be truthful," she said, leaning closer toward him until he finally maintained her gaze, "I flirted often with you when we were younger just so I could see your smile. Well, that and...because I always had hoped you would flirt back with me. But, alas, you never did."

She sighed airily, giving him her best teasing grin. Finally, the tightness in her chest eased, for those words were tinted with the truth. The fact that he would never lower his guard enough to flirt back was one of the reasons she'd never entertained returning his feelings.

Even now, he remained as stoic as ever, though his eyes did not falter as they so often did. "I fear you would not be able to bear it if I did flirt with you."

That was not what she'd expected. She gave a little laugh. "Whatever do you mean?"

With a quick glance toward the door, Dr. Kent leaned toward her. "I'm more than willing to show you exactly what I mean," he whispered.

She watched him with curiosity, his gaze escalating, boring into her eyes with such intensity, she struggled to maintain his stare.

"What are you doing, Dr. Kent?" She shifted in her seat to ease the sudden stirring in her stomach, her smile fading away.

"Exactly what you asked me to do, Miss Lincoln."

His eyes shifted between hers before falling to her lips, and her breath caught in her throat. Was he flirting with her or was he...

Slowly, he reached his right hand forward, hesitating only a moment before sliding his fingers past her chin and along her jawline, settling on her neck just below her ear.

She'd never been touched so softly, so deliberately—particularly by this gentleman. Before, his hands had trembled holding hers during those brief moments of their dance. Now, his fingers held her securely, though with a tenderness she hadn't known any gentleman could possess.

How could this be the same Benjamin Kent who had struggled to maintain an ounce of courage around her, who was now seemingly putting a spell over her?

How could she maintain his stare when his caress was making her head spin as if she'd fallen at the Frost Fair all over again? Or when his lips parted, making her wonder if perhaps she would allow him to—

Dr. Kent withdrew his hand without a moment's notice. "Your heartbeat is strong, Miss Lincoln. Though perhaps a little too strong."

He reached for his booklet and pencil, jotting a few words down. "I suggest you consume fewer sweets this evening."

Lucy blinked. Heartbeat? Heartbeat.

Heat fed across her cheeks like emptied ink on paper, her breathing still shallow. Dr. Kent had been checking her pulse. He'd been toying with her—not flirting with her.

And she had absolutely deserved it.

He glanced up at her with an innocent expression. "And perhaps you had better remain seated away from any fires this evening. You appear a little flushed."

# CHAPTER 7

At Miss Lincoln's deepening blush, Benjamin could no longer keep his satisfied smile at bay. He'd beaten her at her own game, and oh, how wonderful it felt to finally do so.

Miss Lincoln *still* had a great deal of nerve. Dressing nicely for attention, curving her neck this way and that to highlight her elegance, smiling beneath fluttering eyelashes. She hadn't changed her coquettish ways. But he would no longer fall victim to them—and he would be sure to let her know.

Footsteps softly padded nearby as Mrs. Bird finally left her station at the door. "So tell me, Dr. Kent. Is my niece well enough to join me for Christmas dinner?"

"I have wonderful news, Mrs. Bird," he said, feeling far lighter than he had when he'd entered the room. "I believe your niece has made a full recovery and is more than well enough to join you."

Mrs. Bird clapped her hands. "That is wonderful news!" She faced Miss Lincoln. "You see, my dear? It was wise of us to wait until Dr. Kent had given us the approval. Now we shan't have to worry at all."

Miss Lincoln blinked mutely. "Oh, yes. It is wonderful."

Her eyes flitted to Benjamin, and he met her gaze with confident indifference before eying his booklet.

*Heart...normal...red...possib...fbr...*

His writing was nonsensical, his handwriting ineligible. He'd merely been scribbling half-words and letters to keep his eyes away from Miss Lincoln's charms and red gown. Of course, he'd outgrown the effect she had on him. Although, he had not outgrown his appreciation of a beautiful woman in such a dress.

"There will be no lasting side effects?" Mrs. Bird asked, glancing at his booklet.

He closed it before his scribbles were discovered. "None at all. She ought to be able to venture forth out of doors as early as tomorrow, should her headache and dizziness remain away."

"Is this not the best news, Lucy?"

Miss Lincoln pressed a gloved hand to her cheeks, no doubt attempting to hide her blush. "Yes, Aunt."

Benjamin stifled another satisfied grin. He wasn't so naïve to believe Lucy had fallen for him, of course. But perhaps now he'd humbled her enough to have her realize he wasn't that same, silent boy from Fawsley who fawned over her.

After replacing his belongings in his bag, his fingers fiddled clumsily against the clasps. He was famished, that's why he fumbled. Not because it felt as if her quickened heartbeat still thrummed against his fingertips.

He wasn't affected by her any longer. He was a confident, secure physician and gentleman—who was now in desperate need of time alone.

"I shall take my leave now." He finally secured his bag then turned to face Mrs. Bird and her niece with a smile. "I do hope you have a wonderful Christmas evening with..." He cleared his throat to hide his disdain. "With Mr. Carter. Good evening to the both of you."

He moved toward the door with determined steps. Benjamin had lied before when he'd said he hadn't seen Mr. Carter in London. He'd spent his fair share of time avoiding the man. They hadn't spoken for four years, and he'd prefer to keep it that way.

But Mrs. Bird's words stopped him. "Thank you, Dr. Kent, but I am afraid my niece and I will be very disappointed in that regard." She glanced to Miss Lincoln. "I was just discussing this with Mrs. Jensen, including a mishap with half a burnt goose—and a myriad of other disasters with dinner—but that is neither here nor there. The point is, I've received a note from Mr. Carter, informing us that he must cancel this evening."

Miss Lincoln's brow lowered with disappointment. It wouldn't surprise Benjamin if she'd finally attached herself to Mr. Carter. The man had always encouraged her to be reckless, even more so than Mrs. Bird had. What *would* be surprising was if Mr. Carter actually loved Miss Lincoln in return. That man had always made it very clear that he did not wish to marry at all, enjoying the company of many women rather than one.

That was just another reason for Benjamin to loathe the man.

"Did he mention why he could not join us?" Miss Lincoln asked.

Perhaps Benjamin could steal away without their notice, simply slip out the door without a noise. But not while Mrs. Bird's focus continually shifted toward him.

"No, but he apologized profusely and begged to make it up to the both of us."

Typical Martin Carter. Leaving ladies to fend for themselves even on Christmas Day.

Although, Mrs. Bird appeared far more distraught than Miss Lincoln, whose look of disappointment slowly shifted to a cheery smile with a simple shake of her head. "Well, we shall still have a fine evening with just the two of us, Aunt."

Was she not attached to Mr. Carter, then? Not that it mattered to Benjamin, of course.

"Absolutely," Mrs. Bird said. Then her eyes inched to Benjamin's. "Unless…unless we have a fine evening with the *three* of us."

Benjamin stared, unsure whether to feel flattered or humored by her hinted invitation. How he longed to tell her who he was—how she'd ignored him years ago the moment she'd seen his old, tattered breeches and poorly tied cravat. The Kents hadn't much money for fine clothing back then, nor had he any great desire to prance about like other men his age.

So now, to be invited by Mrs. Bird to dine at her table was all too satisfying.

Then again, to dine with Miss Lincoln, to spend the entire evening alone with these two women, would be almost unbearable.

"I thank you for the offer, Mrs. Bird. Truly. But I could not impose —especially with such short notice."

"But it would be no imposition at all," Mrs. Bird pressed. "We were already expecting another mouth to feed. You would surely be welcome. Unless, of course, you are engaged elsewhere."

Blast, blast, blast. Why he told Miss Lincoln he had no other plans that evening apart from dining with himself was beyond him. Never had he regretted opening his mouth more. He should've just lied and given in to her rather presumptuous prying by saying he *was* dining with Miss Parfitt.

"I, well, no, I haven't any other plans. But I couldn't ask you to do such a thing as to invite me to your family dinner."

He glanced to Miss Lincoln, who quickly shuffled her gaze away.

"Heavens above," Mrs. Bird said. "If you have nowhere else to go, then I insist. Gentlemen always make a party far more entertaining. And this is truly the least we can do after all you've done for my niece. We would both be more than thrilled to have you join us. Would we not, Lucy?"

Miss Lincoln had the courtesy to nod, but Benjamin knew she wished him to stay there less than he did. Why would she not, after embarrassing herself moments ago?

"Do say you will stay, Dr. Kent," Mrs. Bird finished.

Benjamin bit his tongue. If there was one thing he'd learned in his four years of practice in London, it was that amiability and friendli-ness—and the ability to carry on a conversation—were the surest ways of gaining new patients.

Mrs. Bird had to be influential in Town. Should he wish for her good word to spread to others, he needed to be all things gentlemanly and more. And refusing an offer to dine would hardly be considered proper.

With a deep breath, he finally nodded. "Thank you, Mrs. Bird. I will gratefully accept your offer. Although," he paused, motioning to his boots and breeches, "I do apologize, as I am hardly dressed for such a fine affair."

"That is perfectly acceptable for the short notice we've given you," Mrs. Bird assured him. "Will this not be lovely, Lucy, to have Dr. Kent dine with us?"

Miss Lincoln's smile curved as taut as a branch weighed down by drifts of snow. "Lovely. Absolutely lovely."

The tightness in Benjamin's shoulders eased slightly. Perhaps this evening wouldn't be so very bad after all. He was already enjoying the discomfort he was inflicting on Miss Lincoln. It might be fun to maintain that upper-hand for a little while longer.

Gearing up for another evening of socializing—as opposed to the quiet night at home he would have preferred—Benjamin followed the ladies down the stairs, careful not to tread on Miss Lincoln's short train, rippling down the steps behind her like a shimmering, red waterfall.

When they reached the landing, Miss Lincoln gasped, pausing in the entryway. "Oh, Aunt! This must be the surprise you were referring to earlier. It's just beautiful."

Benjamin followed her eyeline to view the décor himself, which he'd noticed upon entering Mrs. Bird's home. Boughs of evergreen tied with red ribbon hung above doorways, and deep green ivy swirled up and around statues and curtains.

As they moved forward, the drawing room was even more festive with its crackling fire, mistletoe above the hearth, and candles lighting the room, the holders surrounded by holly berries and white lace. The earthy scent of pines permeated the space, filling even Benjamin with the Christmas spirit.

"Now it truly feels like Christmas," Miss Lincoln said, looping her arm through her aunt's as they entered the room more fully.

"I'm so pleased you like it, my dear. We were able to purchase most of it from local vendors. I know how you love your country Christmases."

They shared a smile, and Benjamin shifted away to provide them a moment's privacy. In all his years in London, he'd never had his house decorated before. He'd never really seen a reason to. But he couldn't deny the nostalgia he felt at such a scene. His mother always saw to their small house being warmly decorated. How he missed his early Christmases with her and Father, before Christmastide became a season filled with painful memories.

"And what do you think of the décor, Dr. Kent?" Mrs. Bird asked him. "Does it meet with your approval?"

"Absolutely. I've never seen a place so festively decorated."

Mrs. Bird beamed.

Good. That was what Benjamin wanted. To flatter the woman just enough for her to recommend his doctoral services to all her wealthy friends.

Shortly, the small party migrated to the dining room. The enticing aroma that pervaded the area spoke of hours of effort from Mrs. Bird's help. The spread consisted of half a large goose, roast beef, brawn, boiled potatoes, carrots, and countless other dishes.

Despite the oddity of Benjamin now eating with Mrs. Bird and Miss Lincoln—who still had yet to meet his gaze—he was glad to have stayed, if only to keep the food from going to waste.

After sitting at the head of the table, the woman took a single bite before directing her attention on Benjamin. "I'm so pleased we were able to convince you to join us this evening, Dr. Kent. Though, I cannot help but wonder how such a fine gentleman has managed to find himself on Christmas day without anywhere else to dine but his own home."

He swallowed his mouthful, taking the opportunity to come up with a viable response. In truth, he'd declined over three invitations from families all with amiable, eligible young women, including Miss Parfitt. But peace at home was far more appealing, even if Christmas dinner for him consisted of dry, reheated meat and a glass of port.

"Christmas day is usually a quiet affair for most families to keep to themselves," he finally settled with. "I don't mind remaining at home."

"But all alone?" Mrs. Bird shook her head. "I couldn't bear such a thing. I always have to be surrounded by friends or family. That's why

I'm so pleased to have my Lucy here this Christmas." She paused to send a smile toward her niece. "Last year, we were forced to spend the festivities apart—a fact I shall rue forever."

Miss Lincoln merely nodded, keeping her eyes on her plate of food. She clearly did not wish to speak further after what had occurred in her aunt's dressing room. Unfortunately, this only proved to increase Benjamin's desire to *make* her speak.

"And where were you last year, Miss Lincoln?"

She swallowed a seemingly large mouthful, wincing. "I...I was in Yorkshire."

Mrs. Bird gave her an odd look, no doubt wondering why Miss Lincoln wasn't saying more.

Benjamin knew why. "And were you visiting family?"

"Yes."

She took a hefty bite of her potato. She must be attempting to keep herself from rambling due to her discomfort. His lip twitched. "I'd like to hear more about it, if you wouldn't mind."

Why was he provoking her, pushing her to chatter? Just to prove the fact that she was uncomfortable?

Yes, that was precisely why.

She swallowed again, glancing to her aunt, but Mrs. Bird merely cut away a slender slice of her meat.

"I...I was visiting with my father's brother, Mr. Lincoln, and his wife, Mrs. Lincoln."

She drew in a deep breath, fork and knife hovering above her plate, and Benjamin knew right then that he'd succeeded. She always took a large breath before beginning.

Sure enough, her words took flight like a flock of pheasants escaping a rogue hound. "My aunt and uncle live in a beautiful area. They and their neighbors hold festivities each night, including a musicale a few days after Christmas. Unfortunately, I was forced to participate. However, I refused to sing, as I am unable to do so at all. I did play the pianoforte well enough, though, I suppose.

"The best part of the evening was having the opportunity to meet with so many of Aunt and Uncle's neighbors. They are all lovely people. The Paulsons, the Michaelses, the Pratts. Oh, speaking of the Pratts, I met a Mr. Matthew Pratt who was a fine gentleman. He was at the musicale I spoke of. He is married now to one of the lovely young women I met. Though, I cannot remember her name. It had something to do with food. Miss Fish? No. Miss Cook or Miss Stover? Or Miss Baker? Oh, I cannot remember. Either way, I was pleased to hear of their union. I was even more pleased to have the musicale end, as I was excessively nervous around such a large gathering of strangers. By the end of the evening, though, they were not strangers, as we all grew a little closer. I really do believe that—"

A barely discernible noise came from the head of the table, Mrs. Bird clearing her throat. Miss Lincoln looked to her aunt, her cheeks flushed.

"Lucy, dear?" Mrs. Bird began, her bright tone forced. "Are you enjoying the meal?"

Miss Lincoln blinked, red painted across her brow. She smiled so rigidly, Benjamin thought it might snap in two like a crisp piece of gingerbread—which, incidentally, she had also smelled of that evening.

"Y-yes, I am," Miss Lincoln stammered. She popped another mouthful of potato in her mouth, and just like that, her rambling finished.

Benjamin struggled to keep from casting a disapproving scowl in Mrs. Bird's direction. Why had she stopped Miss Lincoln? He'd learned long ago, simply by observation, that when Miss Lincoln was left to ramble, she'd eventually stop on her own, though she and her aunt probably thought otherwise. Mrs. Bird was clearly attempting to help her stop the habit, but publicly drawing attention to a trait others frowned upon would only prove to embarrass the young woman further.

Of course, he couldn't understand why people frowned upon it at all. He'd always enjoyed listening to her speak.

"Do you not ever go home for Christmastide, Dr. Kent?" Mrs. Bird asked him next.

He blew out a silent sigh. He far preferred Miss Lincoln's chattering to being forced to speak himself. "I have more of a desire to stay here to help with my patients who remain in Town."

"Ah, yes. Of course."

Thank heavens Mrs. Bird had accepted his falsehood. He did wish to help his patients, but in truth, there were many physicians who remained in London and could watch over them just as well. Benjamin had simply not had the desire to return to Fawsley ever since Miss Lincoln's rejection. He would not have risked anything to happen upon seeing her again.

Little did he know he'd be seated across from her at Christmas dinner four years later.

With the same mood that always returned at such memories, Benjamin struggled to maintain his confidence. Truth be told, he wanted to leave. Not even when the dessert course was eaten—towering jellies, black butter, plum pudding, marzipan, and mince pies—could his spirits improve.

"So tell me more of your family, sir," Mrs. Bird said in between small bites of her pudding. "My niece has told me that you practically grew up alongside each other—indeed, that the two of us have even met—and yet I feel as if I know nothing about you."

Benjamin eyed Miss Lincoln's averted gaze. So she *had* admitted that she knew him, though she'd clearly spoken nothing else about his family.

Well, she may be embarrassed to speak of such things, but he wasn't. He found great pride in his father's work as an apothecary. Indeed, his work had been just the thing to inspire Benjamin to pursue work as a physician.

Yet, Benjamin was not blind to Society's prejudices. One mention of his working-class past and he could very well lose half his patients, and thereby half his income. It was far better to play it safe until he could escape London's inflated opinions.

"My father lives in a modest home on the outskirts of Fawsley," he replied.

"Oh, I see," Mrs. Bird responded, satisfied enough with his response.

Anxious to improve his plummeting spirits, Benjamin reached for the last mince pie on the serving tray, knowing a bit of sweet food would help.

But as Miss Lincoln reached at the same time for the same pie, he hesitated, pulling back.

"My apologies," he murmured.

"Oh, no. You may help yourself to it. I've already had too many as it is."

Benjamin didn't want to admit that he'd seen her already eat three. Not that he was keeping count. Or that he was inordinately aware of what she was doing.

He pushed the tray toward her. "One can never have too many. Besides, I know your love of a mince pie."

Their eyes met, the discomfort and embarrassment finally vacant from her eyes. "You are certain you do not wish for it?"

He nodded.

"Because I'd hate to strip you of any good luck." Her brown eyes twinkled—not in her flirtatious way from before, but in a harmless, playful manner.

He knew of the tradition of eating a mince pie each of the twelve days of Christmas, thereby receiving good luck. He also knew how ridiculous such a belief was.

He gave a half-smile. "Thank you. But I'm not one for super—"

"For superstitious beliefs," Miss Lincoln finished. "Yes, I am well aware, Dr. Kent."

He paused. How did she know such a thing? He was fairly certain he'd never told her that.

With a small smile of her own, she took a bite of the pie.

A single crumb clung to her pink, upper lip, and Benjamin struggled to keep from deciding if he'd rather brush off the lingering pastry —or *be* the lingering pastry.

# CHAPTER 8

*A*fter the dessert course ended, Lucy, Aunt Harriet, and Dr. Kent convened back in the drawing room.

"You are certain you do not wish to stay for port, Dr. Kent?" Aunt suggested as she settled on her plush, red chair nearest the large fireplace. "You would be more than welcome to, even if there are no other gentlemen present."

"Thank you, but I'd much rather visit with the both of you than drink alone."

Lucy narrowed her eyes. That was certainly an amenable comment but definitely not the truth. He'd admitted only moments ago that he did not mind being on his own. Was he merely attempting to hasten the evening so he *could* be?

"Well, we shan't complain with your presence, shall we, Lucy?"

"Of course not. It has been a delight to have you with us, sir."

His gaze lingered on her before he shifted to the hearth.

Lucy still could not believe she was spending Christmas with Dr. Kent, nor that Aunt had invited him. For the briefest of moments, she'd wondered again if Aunt was attempting to create something between Lucy and Dr. Kent. After all, it wouldn't be the first time

Aunt had meddled in Lucy's relationships—like inviting Mr. Carter to Christmas dinner first.

But Dr. Kent was no Mr. Carter, and Aunt had said herself that Dr. Kent was dull, especially when compared to the flirtatious and boisterous Mr. Carter. No, Aunt would not put the two of them together for anything. Of that, Lucy was certain. It was more than likely that she simply invited him to stay for dinner merely out of duty for his helping them.

Still, Lucy had spent a good deal of the evening in silence, attempting to hold her tongue to avoid another unavoidable rambling session, which of course, she'd failed at miserably.

However, her discomfort had given way to curiosity the moment Dr. Kent had offered her the final mince pie. She wasn't surprised that he'd remembered her love of the dessert. Everyone in Fawsley knew, just like they all knew of the Kent family's refusal to abide superstitions.

She wasn't surprised by Dr. Kent's generosity, either. Merely reminded of it. Mr. Carter surely would have swiped the pastry from her and downed it in a single bite.

Experiencing Dr. Kent's kindness firsthand again—even after her treatment of him—grounded her, helped her to forget her cruel flirtations, and reminded her that he was still that sweet, thoughtful Benjamin Kent from before.

He just had a bit more confidence than she was used to.

Aunt's creaking chair drew Lucy from her thoughts.

"My, what a superb meal." Aunt settled deeper into her cushion, stifling a yawn. "I shall have to thank Cook personally for salvaging the goose. Oh, but I do love a good Christmas dinner."

Lucy leaned forward as Aunt blinked slowly.

No, this would not do. Lucy knew all too well of Aunt's habit of falling asleep after a hearty meal. Lucy would not be left alone to her own devices with the physician.

"Aunt, won't you tell us of the Christmases you and Mama spent as children in India? You know how I love your stories."

She'd heard them upwards of a hundred times, but if telling the stories kept Aunt awake, Lucy would listen to them a hundred times again.

"Oh, are you sure you wish to hear them?" She glanced to Dr. Kent. "Lucy's father despises these stories. The dull man cannot bear to hear anything of adventure."

Lucy swallowed that familiar irritation bristling at the criticism of her father. Aunt Harriet was typically respectful of Papa—no doubt for Lucy's sake—but every now and again, her disapproval of his quiet ways made their way past Aunt's usual filter.

Even with her attempts to rile Father up, though—repeating memories from her past, poking fun of his reading, criticizing his desire to remain at home—Father never rose to her words, which in turn upset Aunt more than Father.

Dr. Kent clasped his hands easily behind his back. "Miss Lincoln often recounted tales from your youth to a few of us when we were younger. I would be more than pleased to hear such stories myself."

Lucy's irritation fled. He'd remembered?

Aunt smiled dotingly at Lucy. "Of course you would tell them. Well, I suppose if you both insist, I will continue. After all, I never tire of telling stories that involve my dear sister before she...she changed." She cleared her throat.

Lucy was well aware how greatly Aunt longed for the return of her spontaneous sister. But this time, the mention of Mama was different. There was a hint of malice in Aunt's tone that had never been there before.

But this time, the mention of Mama was different. There was a hint of malice in Aunt's tone that had never been there before.

Lucy tried to decipher if what she heard was true, but as Aunt's tales began, Lucy's focus continually and frustratingly shifted to where Dr. Kent stood. The confidence he exhibited was just too appealing, too surprising, to keep her eyes away from him.

The shadow of the firelight flickered against the angle of his jaw, highlighting the height of his cheekbones and lighting his green eyes like spring leaves in the sunshine.

Lucy had always found Benjamin Kent attractive. All the girls in

Fawsley did. But just like all the girls, Lucy had never felt much more for the man besides attraction simply because he was so painfully shy, impossible to decipher, and, as Aunt said, rather dull.

"But after so long, the both of us returned home, and…we wished to…see…"

Aunt's words faded away, and Lucy snapped to attention. "Aunt?"

Aunt Harriet didn't stir, leaning her head against the back of her chair, lips slightly parted, chest rising and falling with steady breaths.

Blast. How had Lucy not noticed she'd been falling asleep?

Well, she knew exactly how, but she'd rather not dwell on that now.

"This is rather unfortunate. She was only now just getting to the best part of her story," Dr. Kent said.

Lucy glanced up to him. His eyes shone with amusement.

"I suppose *she* did not find it the best," she returned.

Dr. Kent looked away. Was he attempting to hide that much sought-after smile?

They remained in an uncomfortable silence for a moment before he pulled out his pocket watch. Would he leave now that the perfect opportunity had presented itself?

Disappointment nestled deep inside her chest, like a boulder sinking deep into the mud after a storm.

She pulled back. She didn't *want* him to leave?

His soft deep voice broke through her confusion. "With your aunt asleep, perhaps I ought to—"

"Do you still dislike games, Dr. Kent?"

What was she doing, keeping him there for longer? What was her reasoning? Surely getting him to smile had been futile. Playing games or having a lick of fun with him would be just as fruitless.

"I did not dislike games."

She found that difficult to believe. Dr. Kent had remained in the background at every party, either listening to the adults' conversing or simply staring out the windows with a pensive gaze.

"Oh, I just thought since you never played that you did not enjoy them like the rest of us did."

"I was not comfortable in large groups, or with some of those who played. But it is Christmas. I would be more than happy to play a game or two this evening."

Lucy gave a wary smile. He couldn't have meant that she was one of those whom he did not wish to play with when he was younger. Could he?

He motioned to Aunt Harriet. "Shall we wake your aunt?"

She wished very much to wake her aunt, but that would be only for Lucy's own benefit—and perhaps Dr. Kent's. "As much as I hate to think of her missing out on our games, I think it would be better to allow her rest. I don't believe she has slept at all since my injury."

"I'm sure you're correct."

Another awkward moment of silence passed by. "Well, what game shall we play?"

"I could be convinced to play anything. Excepting Bullet Pudding, of course."

Lucy quirked a brow. "Not fond of the activity?"

"Of making a spectacle of myself? No, I'm not."

She smiled, a memory taking hold of her thoughts. "Do you recall when we played the game at the Coleman's? When you had returned from school for Christmas? I was sixteen, my first year out. That flour was stuck in my nose for days."

She ended with a chuckle—a chuckle that was soon forgotten the moment Dr. Kent's lips curved.

He was smiling! He was actually smiling! Of course, to anyone else, the sight would've been a disappointment, what with how small the smile had been. But Lucy would consider this a victory and nothing less.

"I suppose I ought to be grateful the *flour* stuck, though, rather than the coin," she continued.

His lips stretched farther, and Lucy's heart soared, but he ducked his head to prevent her sight of it.

"Perhaps we play a round of Questions and Responses?" he suggested. "That way we may keep your nose safe."

Now he was playing back with her? Heavens, this night was full of surprises.

After requesting paper and pencils from a nearby footman, Lucy led the way to the other side of the room where they were less likely to disturb Aunt's slumber.

"Would you rather write questions or responses, Dr. Kent?" she asked as they situated themselves across from each other at a small table.

"Responses, if that will suffice?"

"Of course."

After tearing their own sheets of paper into six different sections, the two of them focused on their writing. Lucy was finished with her questions in a matter of moments, folding each of them separately and haphazardly as Dr. Kent wrote only his second response.

On the one occasion she did remember the young Benjamin taking part in a game, he'd moved just as slowly. Chess would be torture with him, what with how meticulous he was.

But then, that wasn't necessarily a bad thing, to be calculated in all of one's movements. Perhaps she would not always lose at chess if she were more thoughtful in her actions.

After a few moments, Dr. Kent finally finished his writing, unapologetically taking time to fold the pieces of paper next, matching each one with exactness.

Thank heavens Lucy had learned patience over the years. Before, she would have found waiting for this taxing. Now, it was rather amusing.

"What is it?" he asked, catching her stare.

"I'm merely noting the difference in our methods, that is all."

He remained silent for a moment. "There is nothing wrong with taking one's time to ensure matters are proper."

"I didn't say that there was."

Their eyes met. "My apologies for taking so long. I am finished now."

"There's no need to apologize." She glanced around them for a clean bowl or hat then shrugged. "I suppose we may simply choose each paper randomly from the table."

He nodded his agreement, and she pushed her sloppily folded papers toward him as he did the same with his pristine sheets.

"Pray, madam," he read after unfolding one of her questions. "Tell me this. Do you prefer travel by carriage to all other forms of travel?"

Lucy unfolded one of his responses. "I haven't the faintest idea."

Well that response was far more than she'd expected from him. A simple "yes" or "no" seemed more likely.

She glanced up with a humored smile, but he was already moving on to the next question. "Is Christmas a delight?"

She replied with his own response. "At times, perhaps."

Next question. "Would you consider yourself a wit?"

"I do, on pain of my..." Lucy scanned the rest of Dr. Kent's sleek script then burst out laughing. "Of my mother's pig?" She glanced up with a pursed brow, still smiling at the absurdity of the unexpected words. "How in heaven's name is this a response?"

"It's a perfectly acceptable response." He gave her an innocent look, though his eyes shone with amusement—amusement sparked from his own comedy, which made it all the more humorous.

"Does your mother even own a pig?"

"Is this a game of fact or fiction, Miss Lincoln?"

She set the paper aside, still grinning. She never thought she'd see the day where she laughed at something Dr. Kent said. He hardly seemed the humorous type at all. "Very well. But you really should have told me to expect such a response from you. Are there more like that?"

"I refuse to cheat for your sake, madam."

His face was stoic, but his tone was lighter as he unfolded the next paper. "Are you a romantic?"

"That certainly depends on my mood." She gave a satisfied nod. "Ah, now do you see? That was very clever. The response and question matched up perfectly, did they not? And there was no mention of a pig."

"Indeed." He peered down at the next paper then with a face as serious as if he'd told her about a grave injury she'd just suffered, he asked, "Do you like my gown?"

Though she'd written the question herself, knowing it would be humorous to hear the gentleman ask it, laughter bubbled within her once again. He'd delivered it far better than she had even hoped.

"How dare you ask me such a thing," she read of his own response, still laughing.

Finally, his stoic expression brightened as he cracked a smile. Lines at the edges of his mouth creased, and the crow's feet at the sides of his eyes wrinkled. How delightful his smile was, how infectious. They'd certainly chosen the right game to play.

"Are we ready for the last question?" he asked.

She nodded.

"What is your greatest desire?"

She pulled out his last paper. "None of your business." She glanced up at him with a dropped chin and raised brow. "That one *is* accurate."

After another shared smile, Lucy gathered the response papers into a smoother pile. "Shall we read through another round or write new cards?"

"Whatever you wish."

"Oh, in that case, I suggest we do something infinitely more entertaining. Perhaps we ask each other these same questions but give only our true responses."

His serious expression returned. "I don't believe that would be very entertaining."

She narrowed her eyes. "Is that because you don't wish to ask me how I really like your gown?"

"Precisely," he said with a half-smile.

As he looked away yet again, Lucy swallowed her frustration. She did not blame him for the walls he'd fortified round his heart, nor the constant refusal to tear them down when around her. After her cruelty, she hardly deserved his trust.

But he was no longer in love with her. Could they not be friends, even after what they'd been through?

"Very well." She forced a light tone. "If you do not wish to play along, I shall simply have to answer for you." She reached for the questions before him, sliding them toward her and picking out the first one. "Do you prefer travel by carriage to all else?"

She peered up at him, allowing him a moment to respond. When he didn't, she cleared her throat, tucked in her chin, and lowered her eyebrows. "Why, no, Miss Lincoln," she said, speaking in as deep a voice as she could, "you know all true men prefer traveling by horse, as it's far more masculine."

The last word caught in her throat, and she released a cough. "Was I correct in my assumption?" she asked in her normal voice.

"I suppose. Though your delivery was lacking, I must say."

His playful tone had returned, much to Lucy's delight. "Can you do any better?"

He remained silent, refusing to take her bait.

"Then I shall continue." She peered at the next question. "Would you consider yourself a wit?" She lowered her voice once again. "Yes. Yes, I do. I'm the wittiest wit who ever graced this earth." She delivered a broad grin. "How was that?"

"Terrible." His lips cracked an inch. "And it was not accurate."

"Ah, so there is the real answer. You do not consider yourself a wit. Although, I often find that when one does not consider oneself witty, one typically is."

He made no response.

She pulled open the next paper. "Is Christmas a delight, Dr. Kent?" She cleared her throat. "Why, yes. Christmas is—"

She stopped her own words as Dr. Kent's hand sliced through the air. "Stop, please. I cannot bear to listen to this a moment longer. You'll not only damage your throat, but my ears." A smile broke through his rigid lips. "I will agree to answer your questions now, so long as you do the same."

She gave a single nod of her head. "Agreed, sir."

"And don't think yourself too clever for forcing me to surrender. A far weaker man would've buckled under such a terrible imitation long ago."

She laughed cheerfully. Truth be told, she was pleased with herself.

"All right. I shall answer the previous questions for myself first before we go on. I do prefer a carriage ride, though I am not at all opposed to riding sidesaddle. I do not consider myself a very great wit, but I've been known to outsmart a child or two. And Christmas is always a delight for me." She let out a breath. "There. Now give my throat a rest and answer yourself."

"Very well. I do prefer riding astride my horse to riding within a carriage. I am not a wit in the slightest. And no, Christmas is hardly a delight."

She watched him for a moment, wondering if he was teasing again. But when his eyes did not sparkle and his tone did not lighten, her lips parted.

"You do not enjoy Christmas?"

"I do not believe that question was written down."

"But..." She pulled back with a sigh. "Oh, very well. Though it must be known that I heartily disapprove of your feelings."

"I'm sure you do." He motioned to the other papers. "What question is next?"

She flipped over the next piece. "Do you like my gown?"

She had intended on laughing off the question to avoid forcing him into complimenting her, but as his eyes traversed across her dress, she froze.

He stared at one shoulder, his eyes trailing across her modest neckline before lingering on her other shoulder. Finally, he looked away. "You always did look beautiful in red."

Her heart stuttered at the compliment. She'd received many such before, all very flattering. But this one was different. Perhaps it was simply because Dr. Kent had spoken the words. Or perhaps because he'd said them so pragmatically that she believed he spoke out of honesty as opposed to mere flattery.

"Now you must tell me how you feel about *my* gown."

She blinked, drawing her attention back to their little game. "Ah, yes. I-I don't think I'd like you in a gown, sir."

He smiled, though it did not reach his eyes.

"Next question," she breathed, attempting to gather her wits about her. "Are you a romantic?"

"I think I can answer safely for us both," he responded.

She motioned with a single hand for him to proceed.

"I am not in the least bit a romantic, and you are. Very much so."

"Right you are. Though I could have answered for us both, as well."

"And the last," he said, eying the final paper in front of her left untouched. "What is your greatest desire?"

Lucy had hoped for a little more courage before this question had come. It was what had prompted the idea to answer the questions themselves in the first place. But now that it was here, she wasn't quite sure she could do what she had planned from the beginning.

"You answer first," she said softly.

She glanced to Aunt, whose head had lulled farther to the side, her breath coming out in soft, guttural snorts.

Dr. Kent peered at the paper. "My greatest desire would be to live a life of peace."

She'd half-expected him to turn the question into another joke, but his truthful response and his sobered tone softened the air around them. The fire popped nearby as she tipped her head to the side. "Are you living that life of peace now?"

"Not in London."

He was answering her questions. Why was he answering her questions? Whatever the reason was, she needed to proceed carefully. "So you are not happy here? Even with the successful practice you've established?"

"I am as happy as I can be. London is busy, which I heartily despise. But it does allow me to earn a hearty income."

A hearty income? That hardly sounded like the Benjamin Kent she'd grown up with. "And that is something that is important to you?"

His eyes met hers, as if he knew exactly what she was hinting at. Of course he did. He was far too intelligent and observant to be oblivious to her questioning. "It is not as important to me as it is to my parents."

She tried to do as he did, to piece together fragmented information, but she stared more blankly at him than she'd intended—as was evident by his subsequent explanation.

"I send money to my parents monthly, to help with their expenses. Fortunately, Father isn't a proud man and allows me to help, if only because he knows it in turn helps my mother."

Lucy's heart warmed, as if it had been dipped and swirled round in a cup of warm chocolate. Of course that is just what he would do for his family.

"I also..." He hesitated, eying her warily.

"Yes?" she prompted.

"I'm saving up to leave Town. To set up a practice elsewhere. Somewhere near the sea. Perhaps Cornwall."

Lucy smiled. "Now I understand."

"Understand what exactly?"

"Why you are living in London. I couldn't understand why you'd settle somewhere so...filled with people."

He scoffed. "Yes, I suppose all of Fawsley knows about the hermit Benjamin Kent." He motioned to Aunt Harriet, lowering his voice. "It's a wonder your aunt does not remember me. If she knew how I truly disliked socializing, if she recalled that I was the apothecary's son, she never would have allowed me to aid in your recovery. And she certainly would not have allowed me to sit at her dinner table this evening."

"That isn't true," Lucy said a little too weakly.

"Of course it is. Why else would you have kept my past a secret from her? Why else would you not have reminded her what occurred between us four years ago?"

His stalwart stare penetrated her will, and her shoulders sunk. She could say nothing in the contrary, for yet again, the man's observance was accurate.

With a heavy sigh, he leaned back in his chair, the wood creaking against the floor. "You needn't worry on my account, though. I've grown quite accustomed to others' lesser opinions." He gave a cheerless smile. "Now, I believe it is your turn to answer the question. What is your greatest desire, Miss Lincoln?"

His gaze was resolute, his words final. He clearly wished to speak no further on the subject. But Lucy could not put it to rest. Not yet. Not until she'd said what she'd wanted to say for years now.

With a deep breath, she began, her eyes on the shadows dancing across the table. "I will not lie to you, Dr. Kent. My aunt cares a great deal about status, far more than I do. I take after my parents in that regard, I suppose. And it is true that, should Aunt learn of your humble beginnings—even despite you being a gentleman—she would no longer take kindly to accepting your aid as a physician."

She paused, swallowing hard. "I will also not deny the fact that I have kept your past and...and what occurred between us a secret from Aunt Harriet. Because I *have* kept it a secret. I knew, should I tell her the truth, she would no longer welcome you here, and I could not be the cause of even more injury to you."

Silence pulsed, thickening the air around them when she finally met his gaze. She longed to look away, to allow her some comfort as she spoke her next words, but she needed him to see her earnest expression. Her truthful eyes and her pained soul.

"You ask me what my greatest desire is?" she continued, heart pounding. "My greatest desire has been the same for four years. It is that I might have the opportunity to apologize for the unkindness I showed to you the day you proposed." Her voice broke, dropping to a whisper as she struggled to rein in her emotions.

Dr. Kent's brow lowered, but his eyes remained focused on hers, his shoulders raising just a fraction.

"I cannot tell you how deeply I regret what I did. My treatment of you. Laughing at you."

She winced. Memories of that night flashed in her mind's eye, and she was taken back to four years ago.

They'd shared a silent dance at the public assembly. His family must have saved for quite some time to have been able to afford the fee to attend the dancing.

Dr. Kent's hands had shaken their entire set and after, as he led her off the floor. He'd always behaved nervously around her, but that night was different.

They'd stopped at the edge of the room. Her friends—Mr. Carter included—were behind her, and his own parents stood just off to the side.

"Thank you for the dance, Mr. Kent," Lucy had said, flashing a flirtatious grin. "You certainly are a much finer dancer than I—"

"Will you marry me?"

The words had come so swiftly, so unexpectedly, that she'd thought he'd been teasing. But that was no excuse for the laughter that slipped from her mouth, nor the chuckling from Mr. Carter and twittering from the ladies behind her who had overheard the proposal.

Dr. Kent's serious expression had remained unchanged, though.

"Oh...oh, you are in earnest?" Her overly confident, eighteen-year-old self had been unable to keep a straight face. "I'm sorry, Mr. Kent. Thank you ever so much for the request, but I fear I must decline your offer. We would make a terrible match, you see. I would be far too excitable for you, and you—well, you would certainly stifle me and destroy my headstrong behavior. And I'm afraid I cannot let that happen."

He'd stared at her, stunned. Then his once-warm eyes had filled with tears, and his cheeks had colored as red as the gown she'd worn. Without hesitation, he fled from the ball and into the cold, night air.

Mr. Carter had come up beside her, clasping a hand on her shoulder. "Heavens, how you managed to respond without guffawing is beyond me!"

But Lucy's amusement had disappeared the moment she'd seen Dr. Kent's tears. How could she have been so cruel? Leading him on first with her flirting, then rejecting him so ruthlessly in front of the others?

She did not love the man. She was right to not marry him because she did not want to. But she could have declined his offer in a much gentler way.

She blinked, teardrops wetting her eyelashes as she drew her mind away from the painful memories. "There is no excuse for my treatment of you. I was cruel and heartless. And I am truly, truly sorry."

Dr. Kent didn't speak for a long, silent moment. Would he leave without a word? Would he snub her as she rightfully deserved?

But she knew, even then, he was far too great a gentleman to treat her in such a way.

After another moment, he nodded, his eyes still boring into hers. "Thank you, Miss Lincoln. I've waited a long time to hear those very words."

He said nothing more, but a lightness took hold of Lucy's heart—a lightness she hadn't felt in nearly four years. She did not know if she would ever earn the man's full forgiveness, but at least she'd now done her first step in seeking it.

# CHAPTER 9

*T*he next morning, Lucy awoke bright-eyed and rejuvenated. Aunt had awoken soon after Lucy's apology to Dr. Kent Christmas night, and the three of them had shared tea and biscuits before the physician had taken his leave.

"Thank you both for allowing me into your home this evening," he'd said. "I had a much more pleasant Christmas than I otherwise would have."

"We're so pleased you decided to join us, sir," Aunt had said.

After a lingering gaze in Lucy's direction, Dr. Kent had bowed and departed.

Despite his leaving, the gentleman had remained in Lucy's thoughts for the rest of the evening and well into the next day, when, after spending a quiet morning in the parlor, Aunt suggested an outing.

"You've not been out of doors for days, Lucy. Why do we not visit Barrington Books now?"

There it was again, the mention of that shop. "You know I always love a bookshop, Aunt. But I'd hate to bore you with such an outing. Are you certain you'd rather not go elsewhere?"

Aunt blinked a few times before smoothing out her skirts. "We may visit the teashop, as well. I just know you were anxious to purchase a book for your father."

Her words hardly convinced Lucy, but she went along with her plan anyway, as she *was* anxious to find a book fitting for Papa's library at home.

After dressing in their pelisses, muffs, and cloaks to ward off the frigid winter air, they traveled the short distance to Barrington Books.

"It is charming, is it not?" Aunt asked as they exited the carriage and stepped through the small double doors of the bookshop.

"Oh, more so than any I've ever seen," Lucy agreed.

The shop was not large by any means, but every inch possible was taken up by books. Shelves stacked five layers high reached to the top of the cream-colored ceiling, ladders resting against the wooden structures to make retrieval of the books easier.

Counters lined both sides of the space, chairs tucked neatly beneath them, and a warm light filtered in through the two large, leaded windows of the shop. Each glass pane was decorated with pressed holly and evergreen trees, frost outlining the glass as if nature knew how to perfectly frame each of the leaves.

"Is the shop newer?" Lucy asked, breathing in the musky scent of the books—paper and ink and leather covers. "I don't recall ever seeing it before."

Aunt pulled her eyes to Lucy from the side of the shop. "Hmm? What was that, my dear? Oh, yes. Very charming, indeed. Now come along. Let us speak with Mr. Barrington. I'm certain he will be able to help you find a book."

Lucy followed her to where a man wearing a blue jacket stood speaking with another customer. They waited for a moment before Lucy spotted a young man with a short apron standing atop one of the ladders, threading books into the upper shelves.

"Mr. Barrington appears busy, Aunt," she whispered. "Should we not ask his assistant instead?"

"Oh, I..." Aunt bit the inside of her cheek, looking between both men. "That is an excellent suggestion. Let us use the both of them. You ask the assistant, and I shall ask Mr. Barrington. Run along, dear."

Lucy backed away at Aunt's shooing. What in heaven's name had gotten into her?

With a small shake of her head, Lucy turned toward the assistant, but her shoulder bumped against someone else standing nearby.

"Oh, I'm terribly sorry. I...Dr. Kent?" Her lips slipped into an easy smile as she peered up at the gentleman now turning to face her with a surprised expression himself.

"Miss Lincoln." He bowed his head toward her. "Pleasure to see you again so soon."

Did he truly mean that? His smile seemed genuine, if not hesitant.

Either way, she knew she was pleased to see him. Though she had no idea why her heart shivered like the last leaf of autumn clinging to its branch. She'd spent the entire evening before with him. She'd grown up with him, for goodness' sake. Why should she be nervous around him?

"What are you doing in here?" she asked before pausing. That was a terrible question to ask someone in a bookshop. "I mean, have you any specific reason for being in here? Apart from finding a book, I mean." Heavens, she was getting worse. "Well, I mean, clearly you are in here to find a book. I just meant...Perhaps I don't even know what I meant. I simply thought to ask..."

There was that look again, those twinkling eyes that appeared whenever she rambled. He must think her ridiculous.

"It is all right," he assured her. "That was a perfectly justifiable question. This is one of my favorite bookshops in London, so I come here often to browse the shelves for anything new."

"Ah, I see."

"And may I ask what *you* are doing in here?" He leaned slightly closer to her, the scent of his musky cologne slipping under her nose and mingling with the smell of the books. "Apart from finding a book, I mean."

She smiled at his repetition of her words. "I'm in search of a gift for my father. A new book."

"Of course. I should have known you would not be in here for yourself. As I recall, you were never fond of reading."

"Well, that isn't entirely true. I've always enjoyed reading."

His eyes flickered with disbelief.

"It is true. I just...never told anyone that I did." She wasn't exactly embarrassed by her love of reading. Indeed, it was the mark of an accomplished woman to read and enjoy it. But Mr. Carter had always teased Dr. Kent about his excessive reading when they were younger. Was it terrible to hide such a fact about herself, simply to avoid feeling the brunt of such merciless words?

With eyes still filled with skepticism, Dr. Kent clasped his hands behind his back and motioned with his head to the shelves of books. "Have you had any luck, in regard to finding your father a book?"

"No, I was to ask the assistant while Aunt Harriet asked Mr. Barrington, but..." Her words trailed off as she caught sight of Aunt finally speaking with the bookshop owner, her cheeks rosy and eyes alight as he pointed to a few novels. Was she getting excitable over which books might work for Father? That seemed rather odd.

"I don't mean to be presumptuous," Dr. Kent said, "but I'm fairly confident in my ability to help you find a book your father would enjoy."

Lucy forgot about her aunt's strange behavior in an instant. "Oh, would you be so kind? I would very much appreciate any help."

He nodded, taking a few steps closer to the shelves. "Does he prefer fictional novels, educational novels, foreign..."

"Oh, everything. He reads all books avidly."

His brow rose. "Does he? I had no idea he enjoyed it so greatly."

"Indeed. He is always reading. Usually in his study with his pipe." She stared absentmindedly at the lower shelf of novels, various shades of brown and red perfectly lined side-by-side. "I can always find him there, especially after balls and dinner parties. Or any social gathering, I suppose. He far prefers the company of his books to actual people."

"I can understand that."

Lucy eyed Dr. Kent as he looked away, and only then did realization pour over her. How had she not seen it before, the similarities between Dr. Kent and Papa? They were both often silent, contemplative, and despised social gatherings, clearly preferring to be left to their own devices. Was this because they wished to be who they were without Society telling them they ought not be themselves—book-lovers instead of people-lovers?

With Papa, the trait had been endearing to her. With Dr. Kent, she'd always thought it strange.

But now? Now she didn't know what to think.

Miss Lincoln's searing stare would have melted all the ice on the Thames. But where once he would have died for such attention from her, now he shifted uneasily, for he had no idea what she was thinking.

As such, he needed her eyes on the books, not on him.

"Can you tell me what are his favorite books to read then? Perhaps that will help us to limit the selection."

She finally looked away, stepping up to the books and running a slender finger down the spine of a novel. "I believe his favorites are works of poetry. Books on plants. And—oh! The sea! He delights in reading anything about the sea or those who have sailed. Of course, I'm partial to those stories, as well."

Benjamin tried to ignore her words again, tried to pay no heed to the fact that she claimed to enjoy reading. But he couldn't shake the fear, the annoyance, that she was simply lying to...to what? To improve his opinion of her? To find something in common with him?

After her apology the night before, part of the load he'd carried for years had finally shifted—though it had not been removed completely. His useless heart had agreed to forgive her the moment her words had escaped her pretty lips. Thank heavens his logic had remained enough to remind him to never fully put his trust in the woman again.

Little did he know he'd need his guard up so swiftly, though. Especially because today of all days was merely a painful reminder of what occurred between them—and what could never be erased.

"What is it, Dr. Kent? You seem troubled."

Miss Lincoln's words drew his mind back to the bookshop they both stood within. The bookshop he should leave behind, as well as the woman inside it.

Yet a small part of him—that sliver of his heart that had accepted her apology—somehow controlled his movements, forcing him to remain at her side.

Well, if his heart manipulated his actions, his brain would control his tongue.

"Not troubled. Merely finding it difficult to believe that you enjoy reading as greatly as you say you do. I remember you having the same opinion as that of Mr. Carter."

Perhaps he should've left his heart in charge. Her smooth cheeks brightened to the same shade of her dress the night before.

That woman had always looked far too good in red.

She winced. "I'm certain you recall how Mr. Carter's opinions always sounded louder than everyone else's. And should a person not agree with him, he would tease them mercilessly. I thought to avoid such things by keeping my enjoyment of reading silent."

Despite himself, Benjamin heard the truth in her words. It wasn't hard to believe, knowing firsthand how merciless Mr. Carter was.

"Always with your nose in a book, Benny," Mr. Carter would say. "You'll never marry if a woman cannot see your face. Or perhaps that's precisely what you wish to hide."

Benjamin never gave into his provocation, simply walking away in silence. He didn't see the value in lowering himself to fight with such a brainless oaf.

But for one reason or another, Miss Lincoln seemed overly attached to that brainless oaf. Mr. Carter had even been there to laugh at Benjamin's proposal to Lucy. Of course, it had been Benjamin's foolish idea to propose in front of others. He'd thought his grand gesture of love, his spontaneity, would've impressed Lucy, not invoke cruelty.

Yes, the man had always encouraged her to dance more dances than was proper, to do what she wished regardless of others' feelings —to interrupt others, to laugh at misfortunes. There seemed to be nothing she wouldn't do, should the man ask it of her.

"So you've outgrown your fear of his teasing then?" he asked. When had that occurred?

Miss Lincoln nodded. "I have. He knows of my love of reading and doesn't tease me any longer for it." She focused on the books, tipped her head to the side as she scanned the titles. "He appears to have grown more tolerant over the years, as well. Although, I don't see him nearly as often as I used to. Perhaps that is why he seems more agreeable." She ended with a little laugh.

For reasons Benjamin did not wish to explore, the weight across his shoulders lifted, if only slightly.

"So," he said, desperate to distract himself, "if your father enjoys reading about the sea, I'm certain he's already read *Robinson Crusoe.*"

"Oh, yes. That is a favorite of his."

"What about *The Life, Adventures, and Pyracies of—*"

"*Captain Singleton?*" she finished. "Another favorite. And one of mine, as well, actually. It holds such exciting tales."

So Miss Lincoln *did* read. That was hardly any reason to become excited. Miss Parfitt enjoyed reading, too. Probably.

"He appears to have read a great deal of fictional novels related to the sea then," he said. "Perhaps we will have better luck with a biography about someone who has actually been at sea."

Her brown eyes shone brighter, her interest piqued.

"What is his opinion of Lord Nelson?" Benjamin asked.

"Though he does not agree with some of his choices, Father certainly admires the man and finds his life fascinating."

"I have just the idea then. There was a biography written about the admiral a few years ago by Robert Southey."

"Oh, I love his poetry. They're so wonderfully controversial."

This time, Benjamin couldn't help his stare of wonder. This woman was well-read, indeed. The discussions they could have had when they were younger...

"Tell me more about this biography," she said next. "Have you read it?"

"Indeed. It is thorough and extremely informative. I'm certain your father would find it enlightening."

"I'm inclined to agree with you."

They shared a smile, her eyes lingering on him for a moment before he motioned toward the shopkeeper with a tilt of his head. "Shall we ask Mr. Barrington if he possesses a copy?"

She nodded, leading the way toward her aunt. Mrs. Bird turned toward them, her cheeks flushed and eyes wide when she glanced between Benjamin and Miss Lincoln.

"Oh, Dr. Kent, I did not know you were here."

He greeted the woman with a polite smile, glancing to Mr. Barrington, who looked a great deal too cheery for a man working the day after Christmas.

"I was just asking Mr. Barrington here what books he'd recommend for your father," Mrs. Bird continued, sending a sly glance to Mr. Barrington as she rubbed the front of her neck.

It was no secret that Mrs. Bird had had a miserable marriage. She'd been as vocal about her misery with Mr. Francis Bird in Fawsley as she was about never wishing to marry again. But...the way she was behaving with this bookshop owner was peculiar, indeed.

Miss Lincoln hardly seemed to notice, though, as she spoke with her aunt.

"Dr. Kent has actually informed me of a biography that might suit Father perfectly. Mr. Barrington, have you Southey's book, *The Life of Nelson*, perhaps? I should very much like to purchase a copy."

Mr. Barrington winced. "Oh, dear. I'm afraid I haven't had that book here for quite some time. But I will be more than happy to have it ordered for you. You can expect its arrival within a month or two."

Benjamin tried not to notice Miss Lincoln's crestfallen expression. "Thank you, but I'm afraid I need it within the week." She turned to Mrs. Bird. "Perhaps Hatchards has it instead, Aunt. Would you mind terribly if we stopped there next?"

Mr. Barrington's face fell, clearly upset with having his smaller establishment compared to one of the largest bookshops in Town.

Mrs. Bird shook her head with a quick glance to Mr. Barrington. "Oh, no. I'm certain even Hatchards will not have a copy, should this fine establishment not have one."

Miss Lincoln gave her an odd look. She must not have seen the obvious attachment between her aunt and the bookshop owner.

At any rate, how in the world had such a connection formed? Mrs. Bird clearly disapproved of it herself, or she would not be striving so very hard to hide the fact from her niece.

Silence slipped between the group, hesitant glances between each of them before Miss Lincoln spoke again.

"Well, I suppose we had better take our leave then. Thank you, Mr. Barrington."

He nodded, his eyes sparkling as they settled on Mrs. Bird, who gave a coy smile to the man before following her niece toward the door.

Miss Lincoln left without a word to Benjamin. Did that mean she'd forgotten about him or that she merely expected him to follow her outside?

He really should remain within the bookshop, but once again, his perfidious heart prevailed.

Once he'd joined them out of doors, Miss Lincoln turned to him with a smile. So she had expected him to follow. What did that say about him that he did?

"Thank you for your help, Dr. Kent. It was such a wonderful suggestion, I do hope to find it."

He nodded, pulling in his lips. "It was no trouble. I wish you luck in your endeavors. Good day, Miss Lincoln, Mrs. Bird."

Mrs. Bird blinked, as if only now aware that Benjamin had been standing beside them.

Miss Lincoln, however, narrowed her eyes. "But weren't you looking for a book inside the shop, as well? I'm so sorry to have stopped you in your search."

His cheeks warmed as if he stood too close to a fire. Why had he followed her in the first place?

"Yes, but I was simply browsing," he replied.

Her smile grew, and she motioned to the direction he had been heading. "Are you walking this way?"

"I am."

"In that case, you would be more than welcome to join us. We had a desire to see how the Frost Fair was coming about. Though we shan't venture onto the ice today. For obvious reasons." She gave her aunt a knowing look, but Mrs. Bird was looking through the windows of the bookshop. "Aunt?"

Mrs. Bird turned with blank eyes. "Pardon? Oh, yes. Do join us, Dr. Kent."

Without a good enough excuse not to, Benjamin nodded his agreement and fell into step beside Miss Lincoln, careful to clasp his hands together tightly behind him so as not to brush them against her. Mrs. Bird walked alongside them in silence.

"Have you any appointments to see to today?" Miss Lincoln asked. "Or have you finished with them already?"

"I've one this evening. Though I'm sure another will arise."

"Has your work amplified since winter began?"

He peered down at her, wondering at the sudden questions, but her expression seemed one of genuine interest. "With people falling victim to colds and slipping on the ice—at the Frost Fair and elsewhere—the winter months are always busier."

"You must be exhausted. Although knowing that you help others must bring you a certain feeling of accomplishment."

Now who was the one being astute? "Yes, you are exactly right. I try to—"

"Miss Lincoln!"

Benjamin didn't even have a moment to turn before a man nudged him from behind to stand at Miss Lincoln's side.

At once, irritation wrapped its unrelenting fingers around Benjamin's chest and refused to lessen its hold. Benjamin knew that confident smirk anywhere—that confident smirk he'd always despised.

For it belonged to none other than Mr. Martin Carter.

# CHAPTER 10

*B*enjamin stood back, watching the exchange unfold between Miss Lincoln, who beamed with a broad smile, and Mr. Carter, who had eyes only for Miss Lincoln.

"Ah, I'm so pleased to see you walking about!" Mr. Carter said loud enough for those walking past to watch them with disapproving glances.

He never was one to have a care for others.

"I do hope you took my advice to get out of bed early," Mr. Carter said next.

So he was the one to have convinced her to do such a reckless action? Benjamin should have known.

Miss Lincoln's eyes flitted to Benjamin's then to her aunt's. "Oh, I-I…"

But she didn't have to finish what was to no doubt be a pitiful attempt at a lie, for Mr. Carter leaned toward Benjamin.

His eyes narrowed, then his mouth dropped open. "Benjamin Kent?"

Benjamin delivered a stiff bow. "Mr. Carter."

Miss Lincoln, apparently relieved the attention was now off of her, smiled, facing them both. "Mr. Carter, Dr. Kent has established a practice here in London. Is that not wonderful? I can't imagine how the two of you haven't managed to see one another yet, what with how you frequent Town."

"It is truly a wonder." Mr. Carter eyed Benjamin up and down. "Well, *Dr.* Kent, is it? I'm sorry, but I'm afraid I'll never see you as more than little Benny Kent."

Little Benny Kent. The nickname was only a small reason why Benjamin truly despised this man. It was true that Benjamin had not grown much until his later years, being nearly half the size of the boys his age. But even when Benjamin, six years his senior, grew taller and larger in stature—and possessed more intellect—Mr. Carter still called him the infuriating name.

But showing his annoyance with the gentleman was only sure to give Mr. Carter more of the satisfaction he so desired.

"How have you been, Mr. Carter?" Benjamin asked in a smooth tone.

"Oh, happier than ever, I'm pleased to report." His carefree grin was as annoying as his smirk. "Life in London is grand. Frost Fairs, parties, balls, Christmastide, women." He emphasized the last word with a wink. "Life is superb at the moment."

Benjamin could not even muster a single-word response. Fortunately, Mrs. Bird seemed to finally pull her mind away from the bookshop and focus instead on those standing directly before her.

"So you had an enjoyable Christmas after all?" she asked with a pointed stare.

Mr. Carter, clearly understanding Mrs. Bird's accusatory words, had the decency to *appear* upset. "My dearest Mrs. Bird. I cannot tell you how it pained me to abandon the two of you for Christmas dinner. I can only pray I have not damaged your faith in me entirely." He ended with a furtive wink in Miss Lincoln's direction.

She responded with an amused shake of her head. At least she was no longer fawning over him as she'd done as a young woman.

"Well, after such an apology, how could I be angry with you?" Mrs. Bird flashed a smile. "You shall simply have to make up for your absence before long."

Mr. Carter placed a hand to his chest. "Upon my honor, I shall do my very best. Though I shall always feel remorse for forcing the two of you to eat dinner alone on Christmas."

"Oh, but we were not alone." Miss Lincoln smiled up at Benjamin. "Dr. Kent was kind enough to join us for the evening."

"Did he now?" Mr. Carter asked with a raised brow.

Any smile Benjamin might have returned to Lucy dissipated at Mr. Carter's obnoxious words.

"And we had a marvelous time, did we not, Dr. Kent?"

He gave a polite nod. "Indeed, we did."

"I should say so," Mr. Carter continued. "Clearly you enjoyed your time so greatly with Miss Lincoln you had to see her again today."

Behind his teasing words lingered a strange accusation. But Benjamin would not rise to his provocation.

"We happened to bump into Dr. Kent at the bookshop nearby," Miss Lincoln explained.

Mr. Carter laughed. "Oh, of course. I should have known. Still keeping that nose of yours in your books, I see, Benny."

Benjamin was fairly certain, if Mr. Carter continued to call him 'Benny,' he would be unable to keep from laying his fist directly into Mr. Carter's nose.

"Reading books is the only thing to keep up one's intelligence," Benjamin finally responded.

Unfortunately, Mr. Carter wasn't intelligent enough to comprehend the slight.

He laughed again and turned to Miss Lincoln. "Now tell me, what are you doing walking this way. Fancy another trip to the Frost Fair?"

"Heavens, no," Mrs. Bird said. "We shan't risk Lucy falling again. No, we were merely walking past it."

Mr. Carter raised a finger. "While I can fully understand your hesitancy, I do believe I can convince you both to change your mind." He paused for dramatic effect, worsening Benjamin's mood. "There is an elephant on the ice."

Miss Lincoln's eyes widened. "An elephant?"

She exchanged glances with Mrs. Bird, both of them smiling with excitement. "We cannot pass the opportunity to see such a spectacle, Aunt, can we?"

Within Benjamin's chest, unease swirled like a brewing winter's storm. The freezing temperatures had remained across London, but the ice had to be weakening by now.

Mrs. Bird's brow furrowed. "Is it safe, though, to return to the ice? After what occurred?"

That was the first sense Benjamin had ever heard from the woman. At least her recklessness had its limits when it came to keeping her niece safe.

"Oh, it's perfectly safe still, I assure you," Mr. Carter said, though he had no business of the sort assuring anyone. "If it will help ease your worry, allow me to escort the both of you. With your hands tucked securely in my arms, I can promise no harm will befall you.'

Benjamin longed to share his own advisement, but he held his tongue. It wasn't his place, nor his responsibility, to inform them of the potential hazards of the Frost Fair now.

Mrs. Bird still seemed to hesitate, but Miss Lincoln's sense had apparently fled the moment she'd heard the word "elephant."

"Please, Aunt?" She grasped Mrs. Bird's arm. "I'm certain we shall be safe."

"And you will surely never behold such a sight again as an elephant walking across the River Thames," Mr. Carter said.

Miss Lincoln seemed to be eating up his bait like a ravenous fox in winter. "Oh, imagine the tales we shall tell for years to come!" she said.

Mrs. Bird relented with a sigh. "Very well. But only long enough to see the elephant and leave. Agreed?"

"Yes, of course." Miss Lincoln pumped her head up and down.

"Come, come!" Mr. Carter said with a wave of his hand. "We will be sure to miss it if we hesitate a moment longer."

He offered his arms to both Mrs. Bird and Miss Lincoln, which they readily took.

Benjamin remained where he stood, fully intending on backing away without notice—as he'd so often done as a young man.

But Miss Lincoln looked over her shoulder. "Are you not joining us, Dr. Kent?"

She smiled that charming grin he'd once been unable to refuse. But he was immune to her charms now. Especially with how swiftly she'd reminded him that she had not changed after all. She was still that senseless puppy wagging her tail after Mr. Carter.

"No, I don't believe so."

He tipped his hat in departure, but she frowned, slipping her arm from Mr. Carter's with a reassuring nod to the gentleman. "You and Aunt go on ahead. I'll be with you in just a moment."

Mr. Carter glanced back with a lingering gaze on Benjamin before moving slowly forward with Mrs. Bird.

"Are you certain you don't wish to join us?" Miss Lincoln pressed. "You've no desire to see something no one shall likely ever see again? No desire to tell this story for years to come?"

Benjamin had never been more certain of anything in his entire life. "No, thank you. I don't need such stories to add value to my life."

Her smile faltered at his harsh words.

He looked down. He needn't be cruel to her simply because she was doing the same thing she always did—behaving recklessly with Mr. Carter. "Thank you for the offer all the same, but I don't believe the ice is quite safe enough to walk across any longer."

She flashed a knowing smile. "You were always so careful growing up. Never one to participate in horse races. Never one to climb trees with the rest of us. I thought you might have outgrown it."

"And I thought you might have outgrown your incessant need to follow Mr. Carter's wayward advice."

Her smile faded. "What do you mean?"

"Nothing. Forget I said anything."

Lucy would not forget Dr. Kent's words. She narrowed her eyes. "His wayward advice?" she pressed.

Dr. Kent glanced over his shoulder, as if anxious to leave her presence. "All I meant to say was that Mr. Carter cannot assure the ice is safe. And you and your aunt would be safer to not venture across the Thames today."

Lucy peered ahead to where hundreds of people still stood out upon the ice. Tents were still pitched, and fires still burned. "How could it not be safe with so many still comfortable upon the ice?" She turned back to face him. "Perhaps you are simply being overly precautious. As usual."

"Or perhaps you are being overly optimistic."

His wary gaze was upon the ice, and Lucy's stomach tipped anxiously.

No. No, she would not allow his own unease to prevent her from doing what she wished. Aunt had warned her about gentlemen like him—men who would attempt to suppress her desires to live an exciting, carefree life.

She took a step away from him, frustration billowing inside her like the smoke still pluming from the mutton on the river. This had always been what had prevented her from enjoying Dr. Kent's company before—his hesitance with doing anything adventurous. He always seemed to think too much, only to remain at home, at the back of the crowds, or in his books.

"Don't you ever wish to live, Dr. Kent?"

His gaze hardened, his jaw flinching, but he said nothing.

As usual.

With a heavy sigh, she shrugged. "Well, thank you for your concern, but I don't believe anything is wrong with the ice today. If anything, the elephant's presence has certainly proven that fact. Excuse me."

She walked away but was stopped as a soft hand grasped onto her wrist. She turned, Dr. Kent's gloved fingers encircling her arm.

"Please, wait." His frown was gone, replaced with a look of entreaty. "I...I don't think it would be wise of you to go on the ice right now. The air is still cold, but there has been much talk of the ice breaking apart around the bridges."

She gently pulled her hand from his, mostly to rid herself of the strange stirring in her heart from his soft touch. "Thank you. But I will not spend my life in fear, nor will I be restricted from doing the things I want to do."

She raised her chin as Dr. Kent's gaze intensified.

"I'm not attempting to restrict you, I—"

"Good day, Dr. Kent," she interrupted.

She walked swiftly away before he could stop her again, anxious to feel relief at having the freedom to do as she wished.

But she could barely manage a full breath, as if her stays had been tied too tightly. This had to be a direct result from her confrontation with the physician. Surely not because Dr. Kent's words had been saturated with reason.

She huffed out an aggravated sigh. Fear, worry, overthinking. Such feelings were not welcome within her. She wished to do what she wished, *when* she wished. Just like Aunt. Just like Mr. Carter.

She strode out onto the ice with confidence, ignoring her turning stomach and reaching the others in a matter of moments.

"Did Benny decide not to join us?" Mr. Carter teased.

Lucy took his outstretched arm with a forced smile. The man had used the same joke for years now. Was it still just as humorous to him as it was back then? "You know Dr. Kent dislikes that name, Mr. Carter. Can you not allow him a moment's reprieve from your teasing?"

Why was she defending him?

"Ah, but where is the fun in that?"

His infectious carefree attitude always lent itself to Lucy, but right now, her patience waned.

All because of blasted Dr. Kent.

"I'm terribly sorry again for leaving you both last night," Mr. Carter continued. "Especially now that I know he was with you. Tell me, was it horribly awkward?"

Lucy hesitated, attempting to create an answer before Aunt could think on his words for too long.

But Aunt leaned forward, speaking from the other side of him. "Why would it be awkward around Dr. Kent?"

Mr. Carter responded first. "Well, because—"

"Because it has been so long since I've seen him, of course," Lucy interrupted. "And because typically he doesn't wish to socialize very much."

Mr. Carter looked down at her in confusion, but she gave a subtle shake of her head. She didn't know why she still wished to keep the proposal from Dr. Kent a secret from Aunt Harriet. Perhaps she simply didn't wish to deal with all of the questions.

Or perhaps she still felt nonsensically defensive of the man.

Thankfully, Mr. Carter remained silent, though he still eyed Lucy with curiosity.

Lucy avoided both his and Aunt's suspicious glances.

"I suppose it was awkward at times," Aunt eventually said. "He is an agreeable sort of gentleman, though too soft-spoken for my taste."

Soft-spoken? Dr. Kent was, indeed, more reserved than most gentlemen, but he could not be considered "soft" when critiquing Lucy.

"He's always been quiet," Mr. Carter agreed. "And rather dull."

Aunt twittered a laugh. "That is precisely what I said about him."

It was unfortunate there was such a large age gap between Aunt and Mr. Carter. The two would make a perfect couple.

"Well, it's true about him, is it not?" Mr. Carter said.

"Indeed. I only invited him for dinner to ease Lucy's obvious wound caused by your absence." Aunt looked around to Lucy. "I knew he was far less entertaining than Mr. Carter here, but I do apologize if your evening was not as enjoyable as it could have been."

Lucy didn't know how to respond—that she had a far more enjoyable evening than she ever thought possible? Surely they wouldn't believe her.

Fortunately, after a moment, the three of them stopped as Aunt pointed out a small booth selling books. "Perhaps the book you wished for your father is here, Lucy."

"Oh, yes!" Lucy made for the booth, but Aunt held up her hand. "No, no, you two stay here and converse, and I shall see for you."

Without hesitation, Aunt scurried away, and Lucy stifled a sigh. Aunt was clearly playing matchmaker again.

"So you haven't told her about Dr. Kent proposing to you?"

She glanced sidelong at Mr. Carter. "No. And I don't intend to." Before he could ask her why and force her to answer the question herself, she forged ahead. "So are you ever going to tell me why you did not join us for Christmas dinner?"

He chuckled, albeit uncomfortably. "Never one to mince words, were you? There really was no excuse for my behavior, but...I received another invitation from the Robinses, one I could not pass up."

Lucy wasn't exactly hurt by the admission. Indeed, she'd expected such an answer. But knowing he'd gone back on his word to accept a better invitation didn't sit right with her. Dr. Kent certainly wouldn't do such a thing.

Of course, Dr. Kent didn't like socializing at all.

She shook her head. Why was she still thinking of that man? She forced her lips into a smile. "And what, pray tell, do the Robinses have on Mrs. Bird and her charming niece?"

He peered down at her with a hint of a smile, and suddenly, Lucy understood. "*Miss* Robins. That is what they have," she said.

He grinned in silence. Lucy stole a glance at Aunt, ensuring her attention was still on the books before whispering, "She is the woman you wrote to me about, the woman you might wish to consider marrying?"

"The very same."

"Oh, Mr. Carter. That is wonderful news. I do not know her so very well, but she seems like a lovely girl." Lovely and feisty. With her red hair, boisterous laughter, and loud opinions, the woman had more spirit than Lucy, Mr. Carter, and aunt combined. She would be perfect for him. "Does she share in your regard?"

"I believe so. But I'm determined to discover for certain by the end of Christmastide."

Lucy gave an airy sigh. "I never thought I'd see you fall in love with someone, let alone marry her."

He chuckled. "Well, she first has to return my love before a marriage can occur."

"Oh, who could decline a proposal from you?" she teased. "I expect to be the first invited to your wedding, you know."

He beamed down at her. "The very first."

"Well, there is no sight of the book, I'm afraid," Aunt said as she returned, looping her arm through Mr. Carter's once more. "Shall we continue?"

As they stepped carefully across the ice, Aunt asked after Mr. Carter's family, but Lucy had a difficult time focusing on his response.

For a few brief, glorious moments, she'd forgotten all about her trepidations being at the Frost Fair, but now, Dr. Kent's words were all she could hear.

*"You would be safer to not venture across the Thames today."*

*"I don't believe the ice is quite safe enough."*

*"I don't need such stories to add value to my life."*

What had that last comment meant, anyway? She didn't need to experience certain things to make her life worth living.

Did she?

A low creaking sounded to the far right of them, and Lucy eyed the ice warily. Flashes of her last time at the fair slipped through her mind, but she wouldn't let her previous fall—or Dr. Kent's words—intimidate her from doing what she wished.

All would surely be well.

Or so, she at least repeated to herself.

"Look, just there. You can see the top of the elephant." Mr. Carter pointed forward, and Lucy followed his finger until her eyes met with the top of the elephant's curved, dark grey back, partially hidden by a sea of bonnets and top hats.

"Remarkable," Aunt Harriet murmured.

Lucy nodded, though she was unable to match her awe.

"Let's go over here for a better view." Mr. Carter led the way across the ice, but the view was still impeded by all the others who wished to see the spectacle.

He continued until they approached the Blackfriars Bridge, and Lucy abruptly stopped.

*"There has been much talk of the ice breaking apart around the bridges."*

She tried to shake the feeling of unease, but Dr. Kent's words sunk into her heart, implanting its strong grip into her sense.

"What's the matter, Lucy?"

She shook her head. "I think this is far enough."

Mr. Carter laughed. "We can barely see the top of it."

But Lucy wasn't looking at the elephant. She was peering at the thick edge of ice broken off nearby, the raging water running right by it. Worry swirled in her chest as swiftly as the current.

Mr. Carter followed her gaze. "Oh, do not tell me you're frightened." He clicked his tongue playfully. "Did Dr. Kent scare you?"

"No, I just...am unsure if it is safe."

"I wonder the very same, my dear," Aunt said from his opposite side. She took a few steps back from Mr. Carter. "Shall we leave?"

Aunt was not one to concern herself with matters unless Lucy was in harm's way or if danger was imminent. That was all the convincing she needed. "Yes, I think we had better."

"Oh, come now." Mr. Carter reached for Lucy's hand and pulled her forward toward the edge. "I shall prove to you how safe it is."

They approached a man standing at the edge of the ice, two boys at either side of him staring at the water with amazement.

"You see?" Mr. Carter said. He pried Lucy's clutched fingers from around his arm and moved up and down the ice alone. "It is as sturdy as can be."

"Do be careful," Aunt called from a few hearty paces back.

When Lucy returned her attention to Mr. Carter, he was even farther away, jumping up and down on the ice. "Look!" he shouted. "Perfectly safe!"

Lucy forced herself to relax, speaking calming words to her nerves. Perhaps Mr. Carter was right. Perhaps she was allowing Dr. Kent's advice to burrow too deep into her concerns.

But when she took a step toward him, a loud, dull crack pierced the air, and the ice moved beneath her feet.

DEBORAH M. HATHAWAY

The next few moments flew by in a heartbeat. Lucy gasped as the piece of ice she stood upon separated from the rest of the Frost Fair, shock sailing through her chest and landing in the pit of her stomach.

Shouts sounded around her—from the older man and two boys to the spectators watching with horrified, helpless expressions, Aunt included.

Lucy's first instinct was to jump to safer ground, but her footing was nowhere near secure enough as she struggled to remain upright with the rocking ground. She'd merely end up in the Thames faster should she attempt a leap.

She swiveled her eyes around for help, holding her hands out to her sides as she noted Mr. Carter and a few other men jumping to safety from another slice of ice that had separated away from hers. She attempted to stabilize her footing to mimic their escape, eying the growing foot of water between her and her path to safety, but nothing helped.

Nothing...except a strong hand reaching forth and grasping around her forearm.

"Jump!" the voice commanded.

Without hesitation, she did as she was told, and she sailed through the air, being pulled by a strength she'd never before felt. Her boots grazed the top of the water, her head flying back until her body fell hard against a man's firm chest.

She yelped in surprise, clinging to his arms before the familiar musky cologne filled her nose, replacing any smell of mutton or pork or mince pie.

She pulled back. "Dr. Kent? When did you..." Her words trailed off as his eyes settled behind her.

She followed them to where the piece of ice should have been, only then realizing the man and boys had not managed an escape as they floated down the river on the ice, lying flat on their stomachs.

"We must do something," she said, her heart sinking.

"A group of men are running to the other bridges to see if they can stop them there," Dr. Kent explained. "I tried to reach them, but they were too far away."

She turned to face him again, relief washing over her at her own safety. "Thank you," she breathed.

"I told you it was dangerous," he said.

She blinked, only then noticing his furrowed brow. Was he upset with her? "I...I thought it would be safe."

He shook his head, nostrils flaring. "That is always the issue with you, is it not? You run headfirst into everything without a thought or care."

Her mouth dropped open, indignation mingling with residual fear. She'd intended on thanking the man again, on praising his quick actions. But now?

"It's been four years, Miss Lincoln," he said before she could respond. "Four years exactly. When will you stop behaving so recklessly?" He took a step closer. "When will you stop trying to impress that man?"

Lucy's mind spun. Four years exactly? Since what? And to what man had he been referring?

She followed the toss of the physician's head, finding Mr. Carter laughing with the other men who'd managed to find safety, clearly chuckling off the fear they must have felt. But...were they not concerned over the others now floating down the river? Had Mr. Carter even had a thought to see if *she* was safe?

Dr. Kent continued, his voice lowering as he stared menacingly down at her. "One of these days, Miss Lincoln, I will not be here to rescue you. I only pray you will learn to think through your actions before anything truly terrible occurs due to your senseless behavior."

The breath escaped her lungs. What a horrid thing to say to someone. "Dr. Kent, how dare you—"

"Lucy! Oh, Lucy!"

Aunt Harriet's arms flew in from the side, wrapping Lucy in a tight embrace. "Oh, my darling niece. I thought I'd lost you! I was pushed back with the crowds the moment the ice broke free and have been trying to find you ever since! I swear to you, we shall never step foot at a Frost Fair for as long as we shall live. If anything should have happened to you..." She glanced to Dr. Kent. "You? You saved her, didn't you?"

Dr. Kent merely looked away.

"Oh, how can we ever repay you, sir? That is twice now you've done more for my Lucy than I ever could."

"It was nothing." He took a step away.

Footsteps padded beside them, and Mr. Carter joined their small gathering with a laugh. "Heavens, what an adventure that was, eh, Miss Lincoln?"

She swallowed. He was rather happy for nearly losing his neck—and hers. "Yes, it was."

She glanced to Dr. Kent.

"When did you get here, Benny?" Mr. Carter asked. "I thought you'd decided not to join us?"

Lucy's smile faltered. Did Mr. Carter not know she had been in grave danger—that Dr. Kent had to pull her to safety?

Dr. Kent remained silent as Mr. Carter returned his attention to Lucy. "So, are you pleased you joined me here, after all? You certainly would not have wanted to miss out on an adventure such as that, would you?"

Lucy managed a weakened smile. "I suppose not," she lied.

Abruptly, Dr. Kent turned and departed from the group.

"What in heaven's name happened?" Aunt Harriet asked. "What can he be so upset about?"

She looked to Lucy for an explanation, but Lucy turned away. How could the ice have split off, how could she have been in such danger? Who could have known...

She grimaced. Dr. Kent had known. He'd warned her. And she'd been stupid enough to trail after Mr. Carter, to be headstrong and foolish. As usual.

She'd done the very same as a child with Mr. Carter, chasing after stray dogs, only to be chased right back and bitten by them. Swiping extra food when no one else was looking. Laughing with him at the expense of others, including Dr. Kent, the night after Christmas...

The blood drained from her face. The night after Christmas. His proposal. It had happened four years ago today, on St. Stephen's Day, on the second day of Christmas.

How could she have been so heartless? No wonder Dr. Kent had been so upset with her for trailing after Mr. Carter, with her risking her life. She'd proven yet again that she was still that senseless girl from before.

"Well." Mr. Carter's voice pounced through her thoughts. "Now that the excitement is over. Who should like to go see that elephant? Miss Lincoln?"

Lucy folded her arms, shaking her head. "No. No, I'd like to leave now, I think. Aunt?"

"Yes, let us return to solid ground."

Aunt Harriet wrapped her arm around Lucy.

"Miss Lincoln," Mr. Carter said, his face uncharacteristically solemn. "Are you all right? You really don't wish to continue?"

She shook her head in silence then allowed her aunt to lead her away.

"We never should have returned here," Aunt prattled on. "When it comes to your safety, my dear, I wouldn't risk anything. Oh, your parents will be so upset. Not that I care at all what your father thinks, of course, but my sister…" She ended in a sigh.

Lucy didn't wish to think of such things. Her ever-calm parents would be sure to disapprove of their attendance at the Frost Fair now.

And of Lucy's thoughtlessness.

Though she hoped to leave her thoughts behind at the Fair, they lingered on her poor treatment of Dr. Kent.

How could she ever repay him for saving her life again when she had not changed at all?

# CHAPTER 11

*L*ucy sat across from Aunt Harriet in the drawing room, a blazing fire warming them as they faced the flames with hot tea and mince pies.

"What a day," Aunt murmured, as if to herself.

Lucy merely nodded in silence, stifling a yawn.

"Tired?" Aunt asked.

"A little."

"It is no wonder, after what has occurred. Nearly falling into the Thames would exhaust anyone."

Lucy looked away.

"Unless…" Aunt continued, "that is not all that is bothering you this evening?"

Lucy knew this question was coming. She'd been bracing for it ever since she'd first seen Dr. Kent. And after Mr. Carter's slip earlier that day, it was inevitable. But was she ready to share so much about her past? Was she ready to have everything change?

"Lucy, I've had my suspicions for a few days now that there was something more to your relationship with Dr. Kent than you have let on. Mr. Carter's words today solidified those suspicions. However, I do not wish to pry. I will respect your wishes if you desire to keep your secrets your own. Only know that I am here to listen if you are ready to speak."

Lucy blew out a slow breath. It was time. After all, there was no point in keeping this a secret any longer from Aunt.

Lucy had tried to make her peace with the gentleman. She'd tried to befriend him. And in both cases, she'd failed. At least now Dr. Kent would *choose* to stay away from her, rather than Aunt inevitably running him off.

"Do you recall years ago the Christmas you spent ill at our home?" Lucy asked.

Aunt Harriet nodded. "What a dull year that was."

"I returned home from a ball on St. Stephen's Day and told you what had occurred. Do you remember?"

"Of course. How on earth could I forget? You declined a proposal."

Lucy winced, looking at her aunt without a word until finally, Aunt's eyes widened. "Dr. Kent? He was the young man?"

"Yes, he was."

Aunt made a noise as she clearly struggled for words. "But I...How could you...Why did you not tell me?"

*Because your opinion of him would have prevented me from speaking with him freely.*

Lucy shrugged. "What happened was in the past, and I simply wished to forget it."

"Well of course you would. Declining a proposal is always traumatic for both parties."

Lucy lowered her gaze. In her experience, the proposer had it far worse.

Aunt pressed a hand to her brow. "How could I not have remembered the man? I'm sure you mentioned his name all those years ago."

"I hardly expect you to recall a gentleman four years after I mentioned him."

"What is his family situation? Did I ever dine with his parents?"

Lucy chewed on her bottom lip. "His father is Fawsley's apothecary."

"Oh," Aunt Harriet said in a rush of breath, "yes. Now I remember.

You told me the apothecary's son proposed. That is why I did not recall meeting him, for why would I? Heavens, it is no wonder you declined him."

Lucy hid her frown. That most certainly was not the reason why she'd refused Dr. Kent. She cared not about his father's occupation— or Dr. Kent's, for that matter. She had not loved him, and that was the sole reason for her rejection.

"Oh, I cannot imagine the discomfort you must have experienced these few days past, my dear. How could I not have noticed? I never would have encouraged his doctoral visits. I certainly would not have asked him to dine with us."

Both Mr. Carter and Aunt Harriet had thought the same, that being around Dr. Kent had been insufferably awkward. It had been at first, perhaps. But now...

"It has not been as terrible as I thought it would be," she replied. "But even if it would have been, I needed to see him again. To speak with him." She dropped her gaze, bracing herself for what was to come. "To apologize."

"Apologize? Whatever for?" Aunt's jaw went slack. "Do not tell me you apologized for refusing him."

This was what Lucy had been afraid of, the backlash for choosing to do something right—something Aunt clearly disapproved of.

"I did apologize. I had to. I treated him cruelly. I did not tell you before, but I laughed at him, Aunt Harriet, in front of so many people. Even his parents. I told him that he would stifle me and my life."

Aunt's brow furrowed. "Why should you apologize for saying something that is entirely true? Laugh or not, I see no need in repenting for standing up for yourself, Lucy. He is a good enough gentleman. Respectable, I daresay. And we owe him a great deal for saving your life. But he's far too similar to..." She trailed off with a shake of her head.

Too similar to who? To Father? Her eyes narrowed. Was that why Aunt disapproved so greatly of Dr. Kent, because she'd noted the similarities between the two? Or was it because of his poor upbringing? Or both?

Before she could ask, Aunt continued. "When a proposal is unde-sired, a lady with wealth and circumstance has every right to decline. I tell you, I am glad that you did."

She was indignant, as she always was when speaking of marriage and women's rights. Lucy did not blame her. After a marriage with a man as restrictive as Uncle Francis—the way he prevented her from attending certain parties, kept her from eating certain foods, controlled when she saw her family—any woman would be the same.

But with Aunt incensed or not, Lucy had been in the wrong, and she knew it. "I do not feel remorse in declining his offer, Aunt, I assure you. I do not love him, and it would have injured him far greater had I replied positively. However, I could have treated him with far more civility than I did. He deserved more than that."

Aunt studied Lucy for a moment, clearly displeased with her words. "Did you manage your apology then?"

"I did."

"And did he accept said apology?"

Lucy swallowed. "I believe he did, for the most part. But after four years, a single sentence of remorse can hardly erase the hurt I caused him."

Aunt opened and closed her mouth several times before scooting her chair close enough to grasp Lucy's hand in hers. "You…you do not believe that—because of your apology, because of my invitation to dinner here—that Dr. Kent might perhaps assume that we desire a union between the two of you?"

Lucy sniffed. "No, he would not think that."

He was far too wise to ever think that.

Aunt sighed with relief. "Oh, my dear, it pains me to see you aching so, for something that, well…something that you *ought* to have done. If someone would have told me that I had the chance to refuse a proposal from someone I knew could not make me happy, my life would have differed greatly. So that is what I am telling you now. I agree, civility is important, but what is done is done. You ought to be yourself, unapologetically, no matter what anyone tells you. Your spontaneity, your headstrong behavior, is what makes you, *you*."

Lucy cringed. Was that all she was to Aunt Harriet, a headstrong young woman? One who merely trailed after Aunt and Mr. Carter's reckless behavior—just like Dr. Kent had suggested?

And if so, why would Aunt encourage such behavior from Lucy if it led to injury, while Dr. Kent, like her parents, was the one to advise her to be more careful? Could he have merely been angry that morning because he'd been worried for her safety? Not merely from a physician's standpoint, but as a person who had once loved the *real* her—the person she didn't even know any longer?

Aunt squeezed Lucy's hand tightly in her own. "Are you well, my dear? You look troubled."

Lucy nodded, looking away. "Yes, I'm well. I simply have a headache. I ought to retire early."

"Yes, of course. I will, as well." They both stood, Aunt's hand on Lucy's stopping her from retreating just yet. "I am proud of how you have been able to be yourself these many years past. And for standing up for yourself with Dr. Kent's proposal. You are a strong woman, Lucy. And no one should take that away from you, especially not a gentleman."

Over the past few days, Lucy had thought perhaps Aunt's opinions had softened, that she would be more encouraging of Lucy forming her own beliefs. But clearly, nothing had changed in that regard.

Lucy stretched a strained smile onto her lips then left for her bedchamber. She was ready for sleep, ready for respite from her confusing thoughts.

But no rest came, for her worries sailed about her mind like bats in the night. Aunt had said Lucy was strong, so why did she feel so weak? Why had she been more upset when she'd disappointed Dr. Kent than when she'd done the same to Aunt?

And how could she be herself as Aunt instructed...when Lucy didn't even know who she was anymore?

115

A few days later, Lucy chalked up her feelings of that night to being excessively tired and excessively indebted to Dr. Kent for saving her life yet again. She'd clearly not been thinking straight.

But as Aunt often reminded her, "There is nothing wrong with knowing what one wants. And there is nothing wrong with going after what one wants, either."

Well, Lucy knew exactly what she wanted—for the most part—and that was to live her life unapologetically. Just like Aunt did.

A few days later, putting her usual thoughts into practice, Lucy joined Aunt and Mrs. Callow, a middle-aged woman who neighbored Aunt's townhome, on a walk through Hyde Park. The snow had ceased long enough now for a few of the pathways to be patted down by multiple footsteps.

So often, the snow was just a light brushing, not even covering the tips of the blades of grass. But now, drifts of the glorious, white flakes swept across the entire park, sparkling in the warm sunshine.

"Such a lovely day," Mrs. Callow said, shaking her head in awe as she viewed the sight. "It can be unbearably cold, but this snow certainly puts on a show, does it not?"

Aunt Harriet murmured in agreement, and Lucy nodded without a word. She wasn't keeping quiet because she was still downtrodden. Really. She was perfectly happy. Perfectly.

"Are you enjoying Christmastide in London, Miss Lincoln?" Mrs. Callow asked as they passed by a frozen pond.

A few ducks walked around the edges of it, pecking their beaks against the ice.

Lucy nodded. "More so than I even thought possible." Why did her answer feel so...rehearsed?

"I have heard from your aunt that you've had quite the adventurous time at the Frost Fair. First injuring yourself with a fall, then nearly slipping into the water. Heavens, what an ordeal! You certainly are a brave woman. I'm sure I never would have returned after the first incident."

Lucy's smile felt foreign on her cold lips. That was surely due to the frozen air, not because she felt as if she hadn't smiled in days. She was certain she had at least once or twice. "I could hardly let a little slip on the ice keep me away, now could I?"

Aunt laughed beside her. "That is my Lucy. Never one to be deterred by anything—or anyone—when it comes to doing what she desires."

Lucy couldn't meet her proud gaze.

For what seemed the hundredth time, Dr. Kent's words flickered past her ears. *"When will you stop behaving recklessly?"*

Once again, her stomach hardened, as if her food that morning had turned to stone within her. She hadn't really been behaving recklessly. She'd merely been following along with Mr. Carter. Of course, Dr. Kent had also taken issue with that. No doubt because Mr. Carter often led her into scrapes of their own, but that was neither here nor there.

If Aunt could worry after Lucy's safety and still encourage her to be herself, why could Dr. Kent not do the same?

"I'm pleased you are recovered, Miss Lincoln," Mrs. Callow said, thankfully interrupting her thoughts. "Now you will not miss my little card party this evening."

"Oh, no. I wouldn't miss it for anything."

"Nor I," Aunt said. "I look forward to it every year, you know."

Lucy focused on everything she could to keep her mind from returning where she did not wish it to be. Their footsteps crunched against the padded snow, and a small robin chirped in the empty branches above them.

"We will have such a wonderful party," Mrs. Callow continued. "The guests this year will be sure to bring a great deal of excitement. We have the both of you coming, the Baileys, the Gibsons. Mr. Lampton. And…" She paused, her gaze focused straight ahead. "Oh! How fortuitous. Here are the others who will be joining us tonight, as well."

Lucy followed her gaze, and her heart sank when she saw just who else would be attending the Callows' card party that evening.

# CHAPTER 12

"Mrs. Parfitt, Miss Parfitt, so lovely to see the both of you," Mrs. Callow said. "And you, as well, Dr. Kent."

The two separate parties of three converged where they walked towards each other on the small pathway. Dr. Kent escorted Miss Parfitt with a crooked arm, his eyes jumping away from Lucy the moment they made eye contact.

That was fine by her. She didn't want to look at him either. Or the small cleft at the bottom of his chin that made him look as chiseled as a sculpture.

"Mrs. Callow," Mrs. Parfitt greeted, "it is lovely to see you, as well. We are so looking forward to this evening."

"We were just speaking of the very same," Mrs. Callow said. "I was sharing with Mrs. Bird and Miss Lincoln who would be joining us, and then we just so happened to see you three here."

Mrs. Parfitt smiled. Her hair was as dark as her daughter's, though silver threads laced the curls at her brow. "Oh, this shall be an enjoyable party. Will it not, my dear?"

Miss Parfitt tore her gaze away from Dr. Kent and nodded. "Indeed." Her sweet smile reached Lucy, who found it difficult to not reciprocate it.

The Parfitts were always so kind and polite. It was no wonder Dr. Kent seemed to enjoy being around them.

"Now," Mrs. Callow said, "I know you are acquainted with the Parfitts, Mrs. Bird, but do you know Dr. Kent?"

Aunt linked her arm through Lucy's and gave her hand a soft pat, as if to encourage her to stay strong. "Yes, we are acquainted. I trust you are well, Dr. Kent?" Her words were formal. Stinted. As cold as the snow beneath their feet.

Dr. Kent obviously noticed the change in how Aunt was treating him. He glanced between her and Lucy with an indifferent smile. "Yes, thank you."

When Aunt said nothing further, Lucy cringed inwardly. There was no reason Aunt could not be civil toward him, no matter how protective she was of Lucy. She no doubt thought the physician had coerced Lucy into apologizing—rather than Lucy's own conscience doing the job.

Apparently unaware of the drama occurring before her eyes, Mrs. Callow beamed between her future guests. "Oh, we are sure to have a splendid evening. All of the arrangements have been made. I've even convinced Mr. Callow to purchase new decks of cards for the occasion."

Aunt's smile returned, though rather rigidly. "We are sure to enjoy the evening even more then. But for now, I fear I must excuse myself and Miss Lincoln. We've a few items that need seeing to before we can fully enjoy ourselves this evening."

She pulled Lucy swiftly away after a rushed curtsy, speaking under her breath as they scurried away. "I'm so sorry about that, my dear. I tried to escape as quickly as I could."

Lucy looked away. "You don't have to do that. I can manage."

Aunt continued marching on. "Oh, I'm well aware of that, my dear. Or I would not even consider the both of us going tonight." She gave a firm nod of her head. "It is good that we've learned of his attendance earlier on. Now we may have ample time to prepare."

"Prepare?"

"Why, yes. I could sense your insecurity around him from a mile away."

Lucy bit her tongue, though she wanted to say the real reason for her insecurity—Aunt Harriet's presence.

"You must ready your mind to be near him again so you might not feel an ounce of remorse. He mustn't think you regret declining him, and he certainly mustn't think that you were attempting to require another proposal. That must be solidified this evening."

A heaviness crept up behind Lucy, sinking her shoulders and weighing her down as if she'd been walking for days. She couldn't fight Aunt's desires any longer. She didn't have the energy. "And how will such a thing be done, Aunt Harriet?" she dutifully asked.

"It is simple. You must be as jovial and headstrong as you wish. Men desire silent wives who always adhere to Society's rules. They never would wish for their women to be free. Clearly Dr. Kent is this same way."

How swiftly Aunt had changed her tune. Obviously, Aunt had never seen Dr. Kent as a suitor for Lucy. But she'd certainly never thought so poorly of him.

But what if she was correct in her assumption of the physician? He'd certainly tried to thwart Lucy's spirits ever since they'd been reunited. Or had he simply been attempting to protect her?

With a sigh that rivaled her heavy heart, Lucy nodded. "Very well, Aunt. I will be ready for tonight."

"Excellent. Now, let us stop by Barrington Books again and see if that book has arrived for your father yet."

Lucy frowned. "But we only went there yesterday. Do you really think it will be in?"

"We never know if we do not try. Come along."

"But, to walk? It's miles, Aunt."

"Oh, where is your sense of adventure?" She flashed a daring smile.

Aunt Harriet was mad. But then, so was Lucy.

Or at least, so she had thought.

That night, Lucy donned an evergreen-colored gown that accentuated the light brown of her eyes and softened her skin to appear as smooth as the snow. That was what Aunt said, at any rate.

But Lucy was having an exceedingly difficult time accepting her compliments as Aunt lay in bed in a nightdress.

"Aunt, are you unwell?"

Aunt Harriet waved a weak hand from her bed. "Not at all. I am merely tired from our galivanting this afternoon."

Lucy approached her bed, regret pitted in her stomach. "I knew we ought not have walked so very far. Especially when it was all for naught."

Aunt looked away. "Indeed, it was."

They still hadn't found the book Lucy had been searching for, but Aunt looked far too disappointed to be referring to a simple gift for Father.

In truth, Aunt Harriet had been behaving strangely ever since leaving Barrington Books. She'd waved Lucy away soon after entering the shop, spending the next quarter of an hour speaking softly with Mr. Barrington.

At the end of their visit, Aunt had appeared at Lucy's side as white as her sheets she now lay within. Had the walk done her in...or was it something else entirely?

"Did anything happen at the bookshop today, Aunt?" she asked gingerly.

Aunt averted her gaze, her cheeks red. "Of course not."

Lucy kept silent. If she didn't know any better, she'd say Aunt had taken a fancy to Mr. Barrington. But she knew the idea was preposterous. Aunt, fall in love? With a bookshop owner, no less?

"Now," Aunt Harriet said, "enough about me. I still expect you to have an enjoyable night this evening."

"Oh, but I shan't go without you, Aunt. I will stay here to ensure you are well."

"Nonsense. Wright is more than capable of seeing to me." She motioned to her lady's maid who stood at call with her head bowed.

"At any rate, I'm not so very unwell. Just a little weakened from our jaunt."

Lucy still hesitated. The evening would be far easier to manage now, what with not having to worry about Aunt's treatment of Dr. Kent. But still, without Aunt there to guard her, instruct her, how was she to behave?

*Like yourself, Lucy.*

She shrugged away the thought. "But how can I attend without a chaperone?"

"I've already arranged for Mrs. Callow to do the honors. You know I trust her with anything, Lucy. She lives but a few minutes away. You will be perfectly safe in the carriage until you arrive in her care."

Any further attempts to remain at home were swiftly squashed by Aunt's reassurances, and soon, Lucy was riding in the carriage, on her way to attend the card party alone.

She rehearsed Aunt's advisement as the carriage rolled down the London streets.

"Promise me you will make it abundantly clear you still do not want to marry Dr. Kent. If he believes otherwise, he will obtain unforeseen power over you."

Dr. Kent didn't seem the type to want power over anyone, let alone Lucy. But she'd promised to do her aunt's bidding all the same. She knew how important it was to Aunt Harriet for Lucy to assert herself as unwilling to bend for anyone. But by agreeing to Aunt's advisement —was that not bending to *Aunt's* will?

Where once she'd been sure Aunt Harriet's desires and hers had been one, now Lucy was more than uncertain.

Far too soon, she arrived at the Callow's home and was shown into the drawing room. Thank heavens she knew each of the guests in attendance. Had any strangers been there, Lucy would have been sure to ramble that evening without Aunt there to stop her.

Yet, when her eyes found Dr. Kent, her mouth felt funny, like she'd just bitten into a peach skin with no satisfaction of the smooth inner fruit. He stood speaking with Miss Parfitt, who laughed at his comment.

He used to be so serious, but after spending Christmas evening with him, Lucy was no longer surprised to see a woman enjoying his company.

Was he enjoying Miss Parfitt's company just as greatly?

His bright eyes reached Lucy's, catching her stare. Instead of looking away in embarrassment, she forced her eyes to maintain his gaze. She would not be intimidated. She would be herself. Headstrong and confident. Just like Aunt wanted.

She gave a nod in greeting to the man. His smile faded, and after a brief tip of his head, he returned his attention to Miss Parfitt.

Before Lucy could decipher the swirling in the pit of her stomach, Mrs. Callow came up to her with a warm smile. "How pleased I am you have still decided to come, Miss Lincoln. I was so terribly upset when I heard of your aunt taking ill. Especially after seeing her so well this morning. But I assure you, I will look after you as well as your aunt does."

"That is very kind of you, Mrs. Callow."

"Not at all, dear. I'm more than happy to help." She leaned forward with a hand on Lucy's arm. "Now tell me, honestly. Was your aunt so very ill? In her letter, she did not wish to worry me, but I could not decipher if she was being honest or not."

Lucy shook her head. "She did appear a little weakened, but there was no sign of a fever. I believe she will be on the mend soon. But I've instructed the servants to send for me should anything change."

It was the only thing she could do for her conscience after leaving Aunt home alone to attend a party.

The answer seemed to satisfy Mrs. Callow, and she led Lucy farther into the room.

Fortunately for Lucy, the evening progressed smoothly, even enjoyably. She greeted each of the guests apart from Dr. Kent and Miss Parfitt. Those two very rudely continued speaking together in hushed tones at the far edge of the room, carrying on their conversation with joviality until the games were announced.

Cribbage was the first to be played, and Lucy was partnered with

Mr. Callow, the jolly man helping her win far more than she ever had at the game.

"I'm afraid I did not pull my weight at all, Mr. Callow," Lucy said with a laugh. "I'm terribly sorry."

"Nonsense," he said with a kind smile. "You were helpful, I'm sure."

After a few rounds of cribbage, loo was chosen next, then piquet.

During each game, Lucy looked expectantly at the tables, her heart always pinching when Miss Parfitt and Dr. Kent sat next to each other.

They were veritably attached at the hip. Rather unsociable of them, really. And the fact that they hadn't greeted the other guests was hardly agreeable either.

Of course, the only person Dr. Kent had not spoken with was Lucy —a fact she tried awfully hard to overlook.

When whist was announced, Lucy sat down at the table across from Mr. Lampton, a handsome, single gentleman who asked to be her partner for the game.

"I trust you are as witty in whist as you are in words, Miss Lincoln," he said with a charming grin.

She laughed. "Oh, dear. I assure you, I am not. But I will do my best so you do not regret having me as your partner."

Footsteps scuffed the floor behind her, and Dr. Kent and Miss Parfitt appeared beside them.

"Would you two mind very much if we joined your table?" the young lady asked, her eyes as bright as the candles lighting the room.

"Not at all," Mr. Lampton answered.

Miss Parfitt sat beside him at the elongated table, leaving Dr. Kent to occupy the seat beside Lucy.

Her skipping heartbeat threatened to derail the courage and fun she'd managed all night long, but she would not allow it to. She would behave naturally—exactly as Aunt wished her to. Then she would be able to return home and report only good things. That would be sure to make Aunt feel better.

She glanced to Dr. Kent with a confident smile. A smile that merely said, "hello," and nothing more. Certainly one that was indifferent.

Dr. Kent didn't return it, merely settling in his chair with a soft scoot along the floor.

Mr. Lampton reached for the deck of cards. "Anyone mind if I shuffle?"

"Oh, no, please," Miss Parfitt said with a smile. "I fear my hands are too small to have any talent at such a thing."

"It is certainly not a terrible thing to have dainty fingers, Miss Parfitt," Dr. Kent said.

Lucy swallowed what felt to be a mouth full of sand. How often had she wished for that very same flirtatious conversation with Dr. Kent? Even now, knowing such a thing would never occur between them weighed heavily on her heart.

"You really are too kind, Dr. Kent," Miss Parfitt said with a flutter of her lashes.

"Merely honest," he responded.

Lucy grimaced. Was this what she was to endure for the rest of the evening? Perhaps she ought to feign ill and return home to Aunt.

Mr. Lampton divvied out the cards to the four players, and Lucy retrieved her hand and fanned them between her fingers. Before she could take in the sight of her cards, scanning them to see what luck had dealt her, Dr. Kent bumped his elbow into hers, and a light fluttering took flight in her chest like a flurry of snowflakes caught in a draft.

Dr. Kent must not have felt the soft brushing, for he did not apologize, nor did he react, apart from pulling in his elbows.

Lucy drew in steady breaths, discreetly leaning to the far side of her chair. What had Mrs. Callow been thinking, purchasing this elongated table instead of a round one, like most card tables Lucy had played upon? Lucy and Dr. Kent would have had far more space between them.

She gave a small shake of her head. She was supposed to be behaving confidently, not struck by a mere brush of his arm. She squared her shoulders and pulled her cards close to her chest.

"Are you worried I might take a glance at your cards, Miss Lincoln?"

Lucy glanced up at Dr. Kent, though his eyes remained on his hand. So he'd noticed her subtle movement? Did that mean he was paying closer attention to her than Miss Parfitt?

"I'm sure I can claim to know you well enough to believe you'd never intentionally do such a thing," she said. "But...accidents happen."

She emphasized the last of her sentence with a teasing look—a teasing look that was a direct result from the merriment of the evening.

Certainly not because Dr. Kent was now paying attention to her.

## CHAPTER 13

$\mathcal{M}$iss Parfitt was an amiable woman whose kindness outshone anyone's Benjamin had ever known. She was also beautiful and intelligent with a quick wit.

So why did he continue to look at Miss Lincoln instead? Why was it Miss Lincoln's violet-scented perfume he noticed more than Miss Parfitt's...well, whatever scent she wore?

Benjamin glanced up from his cards, Miss Parfitt's eyes on him once again. He placed the same smile on his lips—the one he'd been forcing all night—then played his turn.

"I heard a rumor about the two of you the other day," Miss Parfitt said.

Benjamin's heart dropped faster than Miss Lincoln's next card into the center pile. A rumor? About him and Miss Lincoln? Well, there was only one thing that could be about. His unwanted proposal.

They shared a quick glance, and Miss Lincoln's eyes rounded.

"Oh?" she questioned in a high voice. Would she begin to ramble? "Well, not all rumors are true, as I'm sure you know."

"I sincerely hope this one is," Miss Parfitt said.

She did? Benjamin exchanged another confused glance with Miss Lincoln before Miss Parfitt explained.

"I heard that Dr. Kent saved your life, Miss Lincoln."

Relief slipped through Benjamin's limbs, a strange emptiness taking place throughout his body as the tension dissipated.

Miss Lincoln looked just as relieved. "Yes, I suppose he did just that."

Benjamin's brow twitched. What else would she call his saving her from death upon the Thames?

"Heavens," Miss Parfitt breathed, clear admiration in her eyes as she turned to Benjamin. "Do tell us what happened."

Benjamin sent a furtive glance to Miss Lincoln. "I think Miss Lincoln would prefer to tell the story."

Miss Lincoln blinked as Mr. Lampton and Miss Parfitt turned their eyes on her. "Very well," she began. "I was merely following a friend to see the elephant at the Frost Fair, and the ice gave way. Dr. Kent was fortunately nearby and happened to help me before anyone else could."

Before anyone else could? Poppycock. He was the only one who had even reached out to help her. Certainly her *friend* had not done a thing.

He drew in a calming breath, his blood racing. He'd been so angry chasing after her, so angry that she'd endangered herself for Mr. Carter, who cared very little for her well-being. Especially when compared with Benjamin who cared so...

No. He would not finish the thought.

"Thank heavens you were there, Dr. Kent," Mr. Lampton said as he won the trick. "I shudder to think what might have occurred if you hadn't been. Is it true two lads and an older man were not so fortunate as our Miss Lincoln, though?"

Benjamin nodded. "They were caught in the current but were fortunately rescued by a boatman at Billingsgate."

"Oh, I had not heard of their fate," Miss Lincoln said, turning to Benjamin with a hand to her chest, clear relief in her eyes. "I'm so relieved they were not injured."

Benjamin gave a short nod. Showing relief for someone's safety revealed basic human goodness. There was nothing spectacular about

Miss Lincoln purely because she revealed that she possessed *one* good trait.

"Now, you two mentioned that you know each other well." Mr. Lampton said as he won yet another round for him and Miss Lincoln. "Might I ask how?"

Was it not enough to simply socialize? Must Benjamin now engage in conversation about his past with this woman, a past he did not wish to relive?

Miss Lincoln responded when Benjamin didn't. "Dr. Kent and I grew up in the same small town in Northamptonshire. Isn't that right, Dr. Kent?"

"Indeed."

"How marvelous," Miss Parfitt said as another round began. "Miss Lincoln, do tell us how Dr. Kent was as a boy."

Miss Lincoln tipped her head, her ringlets falling against her temple. "Well, if you take Dr. Kent the way he is now and change almost everything about him, you will have him in child-form."

Mr. Lampton and Miss Parfitt shared a laugh.

Benjamin didn't bother to hide his frown.

"Of course I exaggerate," Miss Lincoln continued, taking a turn after Benjamin's. "He does speak more often, though, and participates in far more social events than he ever did as a young man."

Of course those were the only things she could mention about him. She didn't know him at all.

"But," Miss Lincoln continued, "he's always had that same love of reading and of helping others as he has now. And that sense of goodness that is so rare a trait to be had among the natural man."

He stared hard at his cards.

*Three of spades. Nine of hearts...*

She really thought that of him?

Without a response, the conversation shifted, and Mr. Lampton brought up the approaching ball the Gouldens were holding.

Benjamin found it increasingly more difficult to focus on the topic at hand, or on whist alone. Miss Lincoln's earlier response nestled its way rather inconveniently in front of his logic. Without his logic, he was defenseless. Without his logic, he might do something he very much regretted.

When whist finally ended with a win for Miss Lincoln and Mr. Lampton, Benjamin excused himself from the table. Fortunately, the winners and Miss Parfitt were still engaged in conversation about the ball, so Benjamin was finally able to slip away from Miss Parfitt for the first time that evening.

He blew out a calming breath, ignoring Miss Lincoln's eyes that lingered on him as he walked over to the refreshment table, void of all people for a moment. This was the only way for him to manage at parties—finding random moments throughout the evening to rejuvenate his spirits away from others. He'd discovered the trick the first year of living in London, and it had done wonders for his ability to last evenings and to be social.

He poured himself a glass of punch, sipping the fruity concoction as his eyes trailed inevitably toward Miss Lincoln, who still sat with Miss Parfitt and Mr. Lampton. The two women were fundamentally different in all regards, not only in appearance, but seemingly in manner, too.

Miss Parfitt seemed to fit exactly what he wanted in a wife, but...he did not love her. And he very highly doubted that he ever could.

But Miss Lincoln...

Soft footsteps slipped behind him, and he turned to find the very woman of his thoughts—his very dangerous thoughts—standing beside him.

When had she left the whist table?

"I never thought I'd live to see the day that Benjamin Kent flirted with a woman," Miss Lincoln said.

Her smile was small as she reached for a mince pie, taking a bite then raising her eyebrows at him.

His instinct was to be silent, to make her wonder what he was thinking. But then...why was she mentioning such a thing?

"Are you overly concerned with the fact that I am flirting?"

She opened her mouth, freezing for a moment before her smile returned. "Not at all. Merely surprised. You were such a quiet boy, as I said earlier. It's just strange to see you so different."

He looked away. "Why did you always insist on calling me that?"

"What, quiet?"

"No. A boy. I am six years your senior."

She seemed to think for a moment. "It's just that, well, you always seemed younger than others because you were so quiet and shy."

He looked away as her stare remained. "Well, as you can see, I am not that way any longer."

"I've noticed." Her eyes captured his again as she continued. "Mostly because of your flirting, though."

There it was again, the mention of his flirting. He took a step toward her, lowering his voice. "Are you feeling remorseful that I have paid such close attention to Miss Parfitt this evening? Was my flirting with you before Christmas dinner not enough?"

The tips of her ears peeking out behind her ringlets singed a bright red at the memory. "There is a difference between teasing and flirting. And you, sir, were teasing me."

He couldn't stop his smile. "Indeed, I was."

"I fully admit to deserving that, though. After all, I was behaving rather foolishly, attempting to flirt with you simply for attention. I should've known it wouldn't have worked. It never did when we were children."

He kept his mouth shut. It wouldn't do to tell her how greatly he'd enjoyed her flattery when they were children. He'd fallen in love with her because of it.

"I always wondered why you bothered wasting your time with me," he said. "Then again, you seemed to flirt with every young man in Fawsley, from what I recall."

"Now who is overly concerned with one's flirting?"

He remained silent, unable to respond.

Her brown eyes peered up at him, her expression unreadable. "You were rather taken with me when we were younger, weren't you?"

His instinct was to slap her with logic. *Why else would I have proposed, Miss Lincoln, if I wasn't taken with you?* he thought.

But her words weren't filled with conceit or arrogance, merely sincerity, as if she'd only just realized the fact right then.

With a single nod, he said, "Yes. When we were younger."

"If that is the truth," she began, her voice hardly above a whisper, "that you were taken with me only when we were younger...then why do your eyes still follow me about the room?"

He swallowed, the tension thick between them. "Perhaps for the same reason you do your best to keep my attention away from anyone else but you, Miss Lincoln."

## CHAPTER 14

*L*ucy felt as if she was floating outside of her body. Why else would she and Dr. Kent be having this conversation—a conversation that hinted at feelings neither of them should be admitting to, especially in the middle of a card party?

She could not concoct a single response to his accusation, for she couldn't deny that she wished for his attention to remain solely on her.

But then, he hadn't denied that he'd been watching her, either.

His eyes swept across her face and lingered but a moment on her lips, sending her heart swirling with...with what? What was this attraction she felt for Dr. Kent that delved far deeper than physical? She couldn't recognize it. She didn't *wish* to recognize it. It was too frightening.

"Miss Lincoln?"

Lucy started as Mrs. Callow appeared at their side with a concerned brow.

"Yes, Mrs. Callow?" Lucy breathed, her voice sounding far too affected.

"I'm terribly sorry to interrupt the both of you," Mrs. Callow began, "but I was just informed that your lady's maid has arrived with news that Mrs. Bird has taken a fever."

Lucy's heart dropped, her conscience pricked. What had she been thinking, having such a frivolous conversation when her aunt was ill at home?

"Thank you for letting me know. I think it will be best if I leave early now."

Mrs. Callow nodded understandingly, then her eyes settled on Dr. Kent. "Oh, but this is providential. Dr. Kent can go with you to ensure her well-being."

Lucy froze. "Oh, I-I wouldn't wish to put an end to Dr. Kent's evening, as well."

Dr. Kent, who'd been ever-watchful through their exchange, gave a small smile. "You needn't worry on my account. I don't have my bag with me, but I can do without it this once. I would be more than happy to help your aunt."

With his generous offer and Mrs. Callow's expectant gaze, there was nothing else for Lucy to do but accept. Though she could only imagine what Aunt would say when she discovered the man had been invited to examine her.

"Thank you, Dr. Kent," Lucy said with a strained smile.

Mrs. Callow walked them to the front door as their cloak and coat were brought to them by the butler. "You will be riding in her carriage, will you not, Dr. Kent?" she asked.

"No, I will follow on my horse."

But as the butler opened the door, snow swirled a few feet into the townhome.

"You cannot ride in such weather, Dr. Kent," Mrs. Callow stated. "You must ride with Miss Lincoln, or you shall catch a cold, too."

Dr. Kent clearly hesitated.

"All will be well and proper," Mrs. Callow said. "Lucy shall have her lady's maid, you see?"

They peered down to Lucy's carriage just now pulling before them, and Martha appeared a moment after at the bottom of the steps, having come from the servant's entrance of the Callows' home.

Anxious to be on their way, Lucy faced Dr. Kent. "We would be more than happy to have you join us, if only so you are warmer."

With a swift nod, he turned to the door. "Very well."

After thanking Mrs. Callow for a lovely evening and apologizing for having to leave early, Lucy stepped carefully down the icy steps before reaching Martha.

"Thank you for coming for me," Lucy said as they both entered the carriage.

Martha shivered. She must have had to make the journey on foot. "I'm sorry for interrupting your evening, miss. Mrs. Bird doesn't know I came for you, but Miss Wright is beside herself with worry. She would've sent one of the footmen in my stead, but she chose me to keep the rest of the household quiet."

The carriage shifted as Dr. Kent entered, settling down across from Lucy and her lady's maid.

Martha instantly silenced, dropping her gaze.

When the door was closed, the carriage lurched forward. Lucy's knee bumped against Dr. Kent's long legs, and she nearly gasped with surprise. Thank heavens this ride would be a swift one.

"Was your aunt feeling unwell this morning, during your walk in Hyde Park?" Dr. Kent asked.

"No, not until this afternoon. She insisted on walking to Barrington Books after meeting with you and the Parfitts. I believe that was what finally exhausted her." And whatever conversation had occurred between Aunt and Mr. Barrington, of course.

The occasional passing light from the lamps outside brushed against his handsome features. "How long has she been feverish?"

Lucy looked to Martha, who shifted uneasily. "An hour or two, sir," the maid responded.

"And is she delirious?"

"No, sir. Though she is sleeping more."

He nodded, peering out the window, though he could clearly see very little through the darkness.

Silence followed until they reached Aunt's home, and the three of them shuffled in quickly to finally be rid of the cold. Lucy instructed

Martha to warm herself first, then she turned to Dr. Kent, whose attention had not once wavered from Lucy.

"I will just inform my aunt that you are here, then I will send for you."

He nodded his agreement, and as the butler showed him into the parlor, Lucy made for Aunt's room.

She knocked softly on the door, waiting only a moment before entering. Aunt Harriet lay asleep with the covers pulled up to her chin. Her lady's maid, Wright, stood beside the bed, a wave of relief rushing over her features as Lucy entered.

"How is she?" Lucy whispered.

"She isn't terrible, miss. I only fear what might happen should she not improve."

Lucy nodded with understanding. "I've brought…"

Aunt stirred, her eyes fluttering open. "Lucy, is that you?"

Lucy went to her side at once. "I'm sorry we woke you."

"Has the evening ended already?"

Lucy glanced to Wright. "No, I came home early to see how you faired."

Aunt frowned. "You didn't have to do that."

"Worry not. I was ready to be home." In actuality, she was ready to put some distance between herself and Dr. Kent, but that hadn't happened exactly as she'd planned.

"Aunt," she began, choosing her words with care, "you've taken a fever, and Wright and I are concerned for your safety. I…I've brought Dr. Kent back with me from the Callows'. He's agreed to examine you."

Instantly, Aunt's nostrils flared, just as Lucy had expected. "I don't need a physician, thank you. Nor does he need to think that we require him."

"Just this once," Lucy pleaded. "He is already downstairs waiting to be shown in. I assure you, he is only here to help."

Aunt's eyes burrowed into Lucy's before she leaned back with a grunt. "Very well. But just this once, mind."

Relieved, Lucy patted Aunt's hand then sent for Dr. Kent.

As the physician looked over Aunt in the dim light of her room, Lucy paced outside the chamber door until he joined her, closing the door softly behind him.

"How is she?" Lucy asked at once.

"Her fever is mild and should remain that way should the proper care be given. But I fear her long walk in the cold has weakened her lungs."

Lucy groaned. "I never should have allowed that to occur."

"If I know one thing about you and your aunt, it is that both of you share the trait of stubbornness. I'm fairly sure nothing you could've said would have stopped her." He paused. "Especially knowing Mr. Barrington was involved."

Lucy paused. "Did Aunt say something to you about him?"

"Only that she visited his shop again. I deduced the rest by myself."

Lucy hesitated. "So you believe that there is something…that perhaps Aunt fosters feelings for the owner of said shop?"

"I would find it very difficult to believe otherwise."

Lucy pressed a hand to her brow that suddenly pinched. Did Aunt truly have feelings for Mr. Barrington?

"Forgive me," Dr. Kent said, clearing his throat. "Such gossip is hardly my concern."

Silence filled the air between them before she motioned down the corridor. "Will you be rejoining the Callow's card party?"

"No, I don't believe so."

She smiled. "Why does this not surprise me?"

He remained silent, and she wondered if he took offense to her words before she caught note of his own nearly hidden smile.

"In truth," he began, "I'm grateful I was able to leave as early as I did. I didn't know if I had another hour or two within me."

"In that case, you are welcome," she teased. "Though I do wonder why you would not wish to stay. You appeared to be having such a wonderful time with Miss Parfitt. Your attachment to her seems…genuine."

Their eyes met. For a moment, she didn't think he'd respond. Was she being too obvious, seeking information about their relationship?

Finally, he spoke. "She is a kind young woman. But there is no attachment between us."

Lucy stared. Was that true? And if it was, why did her heart take flight like an orange-breasted robin?

Dr. Kent cleared his throat, motioning to Aunt's door. "I've left a list of instructions with your aunt's maid to ensure Mrs. Bird's comfort. As I said before, I believe her illness will be mild, so long as the proper precautions are maintained. However, should anything change, alert me at once, and I will return to help."

Lucy nodded, attempting to listen to his instructions after what he'd just revealed. "Yes, I will. Thank you, Dr. Kent, for all of your help this evening."

"It was no trouble." He took a step away. "Goodnight, Miss Lincoln."

And with a tip of his head, he disappeared down the darkened corridor.

Lucy remained where she stood for a moment, the image of his broad shoulders and tall figure emblazoned in her memory until she entered Aunt's chambers once again.

Instead of resting, Aunt was sitting straight up in bed, her eyes fixing on Lucy in an instant.

"You were speaking for quite some time out there," she said, her words short. "Did you have much to discuss with your Dr. Kent?"

Lucy's airy feeling from before vanished, her wings clipped right from beneath her. "No, I was merely thanking him for his services."

Aunt scoffed. "He hardly did anything at all." She motioned to the paper at her bedside table. "Apart from leaving a preposterous list of instructions. I assure you, I'll be far better off with my own remedies."

Lucy reached for the paper, scanning over Dr. Kent's neat script.

*Obtain a tonic for her fever from the apothecary.*
*Keep her warm.*
*She may drink cooling liquors prepared from fruits, such as apple tea.*
*If she desires to eat, chicken broth will do.*

Lucy lowered the paper, glancing to Wright, who stood at the far side of the room, her brow etched with worry once again.

"There is nothing on here that does not sound entirely logical, Aunt," Lucy said.

Aunt remained silent, so she carried on. "Dr. Kent is a reputable physician. Perhaps we ought to listen to his advice. After all, we did so when I was injured, and I made a full recovery, as you know."

Aunt Harriet instantly shook her head. "You obtained a real injury. I have but a simple cold."

"But you have a fever—"

"A very mild one that hardly constitutes the name. As you can see, I am perfectly capable of making my own decisions." Her firm expression landed on Lucy. "I will do what I see best for my own health."

Lucy frowned at her aunt's stubbornness. "And should you worsen?"

Aunt settled deeper into her pillow, closing her eyes. "Then you shall call for Dr. Chelton."

"Dr. Chelton?" Lucy's mouth went slack. "You will truly allow your contempt for Dr. Kent to lead you to call upon a physician whose methods you disagree with most heartily?"

"Yes."

Lucy pulled a face, unable to comprehend Aunt's logic. "Is it simply due to his being an apothecary's son? Or because…" She lowered her voice, acutely aware of Wright's ears practically growing. "Or because of my past with him?"

Aunt peeked out behind her half-closed lashes. "Both."

Typically, Lucy would nod her head and agree with Aunt, or smile and laugh off their disagreement. But this time…this time, she just could not understand her reasoning.

"You needn't worry about me around him, Aunt. I am perfectly capable of taking care of myself. Surely you know this. You sent me alone to the card party tonight, did you not?"

Aunt's lips pursed. "And obviously, that was a mistake. You cannot stand up for yourself around the man. Why else would you have brought him back here, knowing full well I would not wish to be near him?"

"Because I thought he would help," Lucy answered truthfully. "He did not force me to bring him here. I invited him."

Aunt clearly did not wish to hear her words. "It hardly matters now. But from this point forward, I do not want to see that man in this house. To associate our names with his would be a detriment to us both."

"He is a gentleman, Aunt. Even if he was an apothecary's son first."

"That matters not."

Lucy pressed her lips together, attempting to keep her words unspoken, but she could no longer help herself.

She lowered her voice. "Is it any worse for him to be an apothecary's son than for Mr. Barrington to be a bookshop owner?"

Aunt's eyes flashed with an anger Lucy had never seen directed at her. "That is none of your concern."

Lucy looked away with a shake of her head. "That may be so. But I cannot understand why you disapprove of Dr. Kent when he has continually proven himself to be a fine physician and gentleman. He is level-headed. Kind. He's very much like my father in that regard, and that is—"

"That is precisely what is the problem!"

Lucy pulled back at Aunt's vehement response. She had always known of Aunt's disapproval of Father, but to take such issue with Dr. Kent being like him? Lucy could not understand it. How could she despise Papa so greatly when he'd only ever made Mama and Lucy happy?

"Aunt, I don't…"

But Aunt Harriet turned away with a frown. "Please, leave me to rest for a moment. This conversation is futile. You shall see, I will be healthy by morning."

But she wasn't.

Lucy went to bed as she was told, only to be awakened by Martha a few short hours later.

"Wright has sent for you, miss," she said, heavy bags under her eyes accentuated by the candle she held between them.

Lucy swiftly left her bed, entering Aunt's room a moment later to a blast of cold air that swirled around her.

She shivered, pulling her dressing gown tighter around her shoulders.

"Why are the windows open?" she whispered to Wright before shutting the door.

Wright stoked the fire, her hair falling from it's usual-taut bun. "Mrs. Bird requested it, miss. But..." She eyed her mistress with a grimace. "But I fear 'tis only making her worse. She's hardly responsive to anything I say now and won't drink a thing."

Lucy's stomach churned, eying the mahogany medicine chest propped open near Aunt's bedside. "Have you given her anything?"

"Only what she allowed. A saline draught and barley water. They've done naught, miss. She wouldn't allow us to do anything Dr. Kent suggested."

Lucy chewed on her lower lip. That hardly surprised her. But Aunt was getting worse. Her cheeks were ruddy, and sweat beaded her brow.

Lucy knew how dangerous fevers were. Uncle Francis had died of one. Should they leave Aunt's unattended for much longer...

"We must call for a physician," she stated.

Everything within her screamed for Dr. Kent. She knew the man would help her. She trusted him indubitably.

But Aunt had forbidden it.

With a heavy weight settling around her, Lucy stared at Aunt. "Wright, please send for Dr. Chelton."

# CHAPTER 15

*B*y the time Dr. Chelton arrived, three hours had passed, and the sun was rising. Lucy anxiously chewed on her thumbnail as he went about his examination with a bored expression.

"How long has she been feverish?" he asked, standing a hearty distance from Aunt.

"More than six hours," Lucy replied.

He didn't write down any observations as Dr. Kent so often did, nor did he check Aunt's pulse, merely eying her flushed skin.

"I've determined her fever to have been caused by obstructed perspiration," he finally said.

Lucy hesitated. "Are…are you quite certain? We spent a great deal out in the cold temperatures yesterday. I thought perhaps that was…"

She trailed off when his condemning eyes found hers. Clearly, it was not her place to question his diagnosis.

"Whatever be the reason," he said pointedly, "bleeding and sweating will be just the thing to relieve her of the fever."

Lucy's heart dropped. This was what she'd been afraid of—this was what Aunt despised.

Aunt Harriet had not been remorseful when Uncle Francis had

died, but she believed her husband lost his life mostly due to the bleeding that had occurred by a physician in Fawsley.

How could Lucy subject her to such treatment she disapproved of? Yet, what else could be done? Aunt had demanded they call for Dr. Chelton.

"Are you certain there is not another way—"

"I do not take kindly to others questioning my practices, Miss Lincoln," Dr. Chelton interrupted, moving toward the door. "But it is ultimately your decision to trust the advisements of a knowledgeable physician or to risk your dear aunt's life."

Lucy did not appreciate being snapped at, but her concern for Aunt Harriet outweighed her desire to retaliate. Surely Aunt would know Dr. Chelton—like so many physicians—would suggest bleeding. Otherwise she would not have asked him to be used, would she have?

Dr. Chelton pulled out his pocket watch with an impatient huff. "What is your decision, Miss Lincoln? Shall I send for the surgeon?"

Lucy knew what *her* decision was. But it was not hers to make. With a wary heart, she nodded. "Yes, sir. Aunt told us to do as you would suggest, so please, send for the surgeon."

He raised his chin. "Very well. He shall be here soon to carry about the business. Good day."

He departed with a curt nod, and Lucy was left alone with burgeoning regret.

The surgeon took longer than even Dr. Chelton had to arrive, coming hours after luncheon to perform his duty. Aunt Harriet had merely moaned and stirred through the bleeding and subsequent bandaging of her arm. The surgeon then covered her from head to toe with mounds of blankets and offered Aunt spirits to sweat the heat from her body.

Lucy's tears threatened to spill down her cheeks during his visit and after the surgeon finally left. She shouldn't have done this. She never should have allowed Dr. Chelton to even step foot in the house.

Aunt tried to remove the blankets in her feverish state, sweat pooling across her brow and cheeks seemingly as hot as the blazing fire.

"She looks awful uncomfortable, miss," Wright said beside her in a worried tone. "Ought we not take the blankets off for just a moment?"

Lucy sighed, pacing the floor at the foot of Aunt's bed. "I don't know. The surgeon said to keep them on her for hours, in order for the sweating to help her."

"And if it doesn't help her?"

Swallowing, Lucy shrugged. "I suppose we ask for Dr. Chelton to return?"

She ended in a question, hoping, praying Wright would say something in the contrary to give her the confidence she needed to defy Aunt's wishes. But the lady's maid stayed silent.

Over the next few hours, Aunt's state only worsened as she lay in bed, unmoving. Lucy relieved the contents of her stomach at one point, fear over her aunt's well-being upsetting her to the point of hardly being able to function.

Finally, they sent once more for Dr. Chelton, who arrived well after dark.

"Let us see how she fairs," he said, stifling a small burp.

Lucy eyed him with barely hidden disgust. Clearly—due to the food still in his teeth—he had to finish his dinner before arriving to care for a dying patient.

"I'm quite pleased with the progress she's made," Dr. Chelton said.

She stared at him, dumbfounded. "She's made little progress at all, though, sir."

"That is because another sweating is in order. And bleeding."

No matter what Aunt thought of Dr. Kent, no matter her qualms that he was too similar to Father, Benjamin Kent was far, far better than Dr. Chelton.

And Lucy was finished.

With insides curdling like days-old milk, she drew in all her confidence. Dr. Kent had been right before. She *was* headstrong and silly and made decisions that hurt others.

But this time…this time, she would make the right decision.

"No, Dr. Chelton."

His eyes whipped toward hers. "Pardon?"

His surprise gave her just the boost of confidence she needed. "I will not be subjecting Aunt to any more of your treatments. Thank you for your attempts at helping her, but we are no longer in need of your services."

He sputtered, but she held strong until he sent her a withering scowl and darted from the room.

"Wright?" Lucy called.

The woman was at her side in a moment, eyes alight with more life than they had been for hours. "Yes, miss?"

"Please send for Dr. Kent."

"Yes, miss!" She left the room directly, her voice filled with relief.

But Lucy felt anything but relief. Not only was she going against Aunt's express desires, but she'd also gone against Dr. Kent's earlier advisement. Would he berate her? Criticize her foolish behavior? Tell her that Aunt was past saving?

She did not have to wonder for long, for merely a half hour later when midnight chimed on the clock downstairs, Dr. Kent was shown into the room. He marched forth, removing his coat and setting it atop a nearby chair with his hat. He must not have waited for the butler to take them from him.

"How long has she been like this? Delirious, I mean." He pulled his gloves off his hands one by one as he took in the state of his patient.

"Since this afternoon," Lucy replied, wringing her hands at his urgency. Was Aunt worse than she had thought?

He didn't respond, washing his hands at the nearby basin before moving to Aunt and shifting aside the blankets to check her pulse. His hair fell over his brow, dark circles beneath his eyes. Had he been awakened from a deep slumber to come to their rescue?

"What has been done to help her?" he asked.

"Dr. Chelton had the surgeon bleed and sweat her, but she only worsened."

He lifted the arm of her dressing gown to reveal the grey bandage the surgeon left behind on her arm. "And what from my own list?"

Her cheeks burned. "Aunt did not wish to receive any of your treatments."

He paused, lowering Aunt Harriet's arm to the bed and turning to face Lucy with a serious expression. "Miss Lincoln, I am well aware that Mrs. Bird must have recently learned of my past—or of my proposal—to have suddenly earned this great disdain for me. But I will be frank with you. I fear for her life. Her heart has been greatly weakened by the bleeding and prolonged fever. If this continues much longer, she will not outlive the night."

Lucy had known such an outcome was possible, but hearing the words aloud, the gravity of the situation slipped past her defenses and right into her heart. She nodded her understanding, tears springing to her eyes.

"As she is far too ill to decline my help now, it is up to you to decide what must be done," Dr. Kent finished.

Lucy did not hesitate. "I have already made my decision, sir. Please, help my aunt."

Without missing a beat, Dr. Kent made for Aunt Harriet. "Help me remove the blankets. We must allow nature to take its course and observe what her body needs. Should she shiver, we will cover her again, but if she sweats, we are merely keeping the heat in her body when it needs to leave."

Lucy and Wright went straight to removing all but one of the blankets, and Aunt seemed to breathe easier at once.

"I assume Dr. Chelton offered her undiluted spirits?"

Lucy nodded, grimacing.

Dr. Kent's only reaction was a twitch of his jaw. "That will only prove to heat her body more. Has she had anything else? A tonic, perhaps?"

She hung her head. "No, not in the last four hours."

With no censure, he nodded. "An apple tea will help."

Lucy turned to Wright, but she was already sending Martha out the door with the order.

Dr. Kent wrung out a cloth at the bedside table, placing it on Aunt's brow. Lucy stared, trying to hide her amazement. Many physicians did not do such things for their patients, leaving family members or surgeons to do most of the work. Of course Dr. Kent would do the opposite.

Within the hour, a tincture had been provided by a helpful apothecary, and Lucy and Dr. Kent worked together to rouse Aunt enough to drink a sip or two of the tea and tonic.

Every quarter hour, they did the very same. Dr. Kent monitored her heartbeat while Lucy and Wright worked together to see if Aunt needed more blankets or less. Finally, after hours of watching, Aunt's fever broke, and she fell into a peaceful sleep, her body no doubt exhausted from combating such a fierce illness.

"Her heartbeat is still faint, but it is a great deal stronger than before." Dr. Kent tucked his pocket watch back into his waistcoat. He'd long since removed his jacket and rolled up the sleeves of his white shirt. "I do believe the worst is behind her."

Lucy sighed, the strain from the last day and a half finally relenting its grip on her nerves. "You are certain?"

He gave her an encouraging smile. "I am."

Had Dr. Chelton said such words, she would have never believed him. But with Dr. Kent, hope filled her soul. "I cannot thank you enough. I truly don't know what we would've done without your help."

She turned to Wright, expecting her to join in with her own gratitude, but the poor woman's head lolled to the side as she sat fast asleep on the chair beside her mistress.

Lucy couldn't blame her. It had to be nearing four o'clock in the morning.

"It's been a long day for us, I'm afraid," she said.

"Have you slept at all?"

Lucy shrugged. "For a few hours here and there."

"Then you ought to follow her example." His footsteps echoed in the stillness of the room as he draped his coat and jacket over his arm, holding his hat and gloves in his opposite hand. "I've an early appointment this morning that I cannot miss. I would not leave unless I was certain of your aunt's safety, but should you need me to stay…"

She shook her head. "No, no. I will, of course, send for you if her fever returns, but you need sleep, too. I am sorry for bringing you out here so late."

They walked to the door, and Lucy did her best to ignore her disappointment over the gentleman leaving. He had been there for long enough, she supposed, and Aunt was not his only patient.

He opened the door, stepping outside of Aunt's chambers. "You did the right thing by sending for me, Miss Lincoln, though I'm certain you think otherwise."

She followed him into the corridor, closing the door behind her with a soft click. "In truth, I don't. Perhaps I did before, as I feared Aunt's disapproval. But now, I only regret not having you come sooner."

He remained silent, no doubt contemplating yet again how reckless she was.

"Would you like a cup of tea before you leave?" she offered.

"Thank you, but I must return home."

She nodded, understanding at once. "I will walk you to the door then."

Most of the servants had gone to sleep as Aunt's fever had broken, though the butler, housekeeper, and cook would now be in the kitchen, no doubt sipping a soothing cup of tea as they awaited anything else that might be required of them.

But the corridors were empty as Lucy and Dr. Kent's padded footsteps echoed on the rug in the silent house.

"I suspect your aunt will not wish me to return, but if I may suggest a plan for her to recover fully?"

"Yes, please, do."

"I would advise her to remain in bed for at least a day or two. Moderate exercise will be beneficial, but she must avoid any great fatigue. She must also be provided with a light but nourishing diet."

Lucy rehearsed the list in her mind until it solidified. "I will see to them all being accomplished. Even if Aunt heartily protests, which I fully expect her to do."

They turned down the next corridor, the events of the day resting heavily on her mind. "May I ask you a question, Dr. Kent?"

"Of course."

"How do you remain so calm while under such pressure?"

He was silent for a moment. "What do you mean?"

"I've seen you in a number of emotionally compromising situations of late, but you never seem to lose control of yourself or your actions. I merely wonder how you are able to do that."

They reached the stairs, but instead of proceeding down them, she paused at the top beside him, peering up at him as she awaited his answer.

"I suppose I've simply had many years of practice," he finally said. "There have been moments, especially in my first year as a physician, where my nerves have gotten the better of me. But I simply remind myself to think logically, remember my observations and the things I've learned, and proceed with caution and a clear plan."

Her shoulders fell. "It is all very methodical with you then?"

"Is that so terrible?"

"For me it is."

His brow furrowed, and she realized how her words could be misconstrued. "No, I meant that, well…no, it is not a terrible thing to be methodical. In fact, it is the opposite of being terrible. I was just thinking of how *I* am not methodical, so I have simply no hope in ever being as level-headed as you are."

She smoothed a finger over the circular wood at the top of the stair railing. "I cannot think of a time before this evening where I have actually considered the consequences of my actions before proceeding."

He watched her. "Have you always wished to be more thoughtful in your approach to certain things?"

She sighed. She wasn't sure she had the energy to proceed with this conversation now that she had started it. She made her way down the staircase, her own weary body protesting with each step. But her tongue seemed more than willing to continue.

"In truth, I have never thought about it until after what you said to me at the Frost Fair, when you pulled me from the drifting ice."

He followed her down the stairs, one step behind her on the opposite side. "I never should have spoken so harshly. It was not my place to criticize you for behaving differently than I do."

She held up a soft hand before he could continue—or worse, apologize. "Please, do not regret your words. I admit, they were not what I wished to hear in that moment, but I've had time to consider what you said, and I've realized you spoke the truth. I'm far too headstrong for my own good."

They reached the bottom of the stairs, and she paused again. "How I've managed to outlive my own stupidity is beyond me."

She shook her head, facing him squarely. A single candle burned near the doorway, no doubt left there by the butler. "But after tonight, after seeing how it felt to actually think through my actions, I can honestly say I never wish to go back to how I was. That is why I've made the decision right now to *never* make a poor decision again."

# CHAPTER 16

*L*ucy had expected perhaps a proud smile or a declaration of how impressed Dr. Kent was as she announced her decision.

What she didn't expect—and exactly what she received—was his soft laughter.

She frowned. "Why do you laugh? Do you not believe me?"

"I do apologize. It is just that, well, you can't even make a good decision right now about making good decisions."

She paused, thinking through his words. Heavens, he was right again. She'd made her decision to never make a poor decision again so impulsively that she'd hardly realized it was a poor decision!

As the words settled around her, she flapped her arms upon her sides. "Well, then there is no hope for me." She gave a heavy sigh then sank onto the second step, resting her chin in her palms. "No hope at all."

This time, Dr. Kent did not laugh. "There is always hope."

She stared up at him still standing before her. "How can you say such a thing? In the last week, I've endangered my own life twice now, and tonight, my aunt's. I should just be locked away to prevent myself from ever hurting anyone again."

"That is hardly a plausible thing to do."

She shrugged. "It is the *safe* thing to do."

"If you had locked yourself away, your aunt still would have made the decision to have Dr. Chelton come this evening," he said softly. "You very well could have saved her life."

"You are the one to have done the saving, sir. I can only thank my common sense for joining me temporarily, as I doubt its presence will remain permanent. My spontaneity, however, will be my constant, afflicting companion."

"Forgive me, but I never suggested…why must you be rid of all of your spontaneity?"

She peered up at him, candlelight flickering against half his face. "You told me if I did not begin to think about my actions beforehand, others would become injured."

He grimaced. With a sigh, he settled on the stairs beside her, readjusting his belongings between him and the wall. "I spoke those words out of anger, and that anger stemmed from fear. Fear for your safety."

Lucy looked over at him, her heart stuttering at their proximity, though they still did not touch.

Dr. Kent leaned slightly forward, resting his elbows on his knees. As he spoke, her eyes trailed over his broad shoulders accentuated by his dark waistcoat.

"My pride had convinced me that day that my own methodical approach to life was the only way to live. I've always struggled with spontaneity myself, fearing repercussions and consequences of each of my actions too greatly to behave in any other way." He looked over at her, his gaze soft. "But that is how I choose to live *my* life, and it makes me happy. I never should have hinted for you to do the same. In truth, I envy your spirit, your determination to enjoy life to its fullest without worry. It is not anyone's place—especially mine as a gentleman of no consequence to you—to tell you what to do or how to live your life. That ought to be your decision, and your decision alone."

Lucy had never felt such warmth lacing throughout every ounce of her body. She very well could have had a cup of tea or be sitting in front of the fire, so happy, so content his words had made her.

So often, her parents had encouraged her to live the way she wished to live. But she'd been so caught up in following Aunt's ways and Mr. Carter's ways that she forgot about her *own* way.

"Thank you," she said softly. "You've no idea how greatly I needed to hear those words. However..." She waited to continue until his eyes met hers. "I must correct you in one regard. You are *anything* but a gentleman of no consequence to me. Surely you can see how I value your opinion?"

His eyes held a level of mistrust she could not fault him for. "Why is that?"

His question had come so softly, she wasn't entirely sure he'd asked it. In truth, she almost pretended she hadn't heard him, if only to quell her rising discomfort.

Surely she could come up with a response. Why *did* she value his opinion? She could just say a single phrase. A single word, even.

But the more she scrambled, the more her mind emptied until her tongue was let off its leash.

"That is a difficult question you ask, sir, for there are many reasons. But where to begin?"

She ought to stop right there. It would be perfect.

"I suppose I value your opinion because we are friends. I mean, I assume we are friends. I'd like to *think* we are friends. Although, after what I did to you, I would not doubt if you did not wish to be near me, let alone speak with me."

Heavens, why was she bringing up such a thing now? Were they not past this?

"But I suppose you are speaking with me now, so perhaps you have forgiven me," she continued. "Not that I wish to pressure you. Or push you into doing something you do not wish to do. At any rate, I value your opinion because you are such a wise individual, like my father. He always gives sound advice. You know, the two of you are quite similar. Both of you enjoy reading, despise socializing, think through things in an intelligent manner. It is unfortunate I did not inherit some of Father's traits."

She broke off with a nervous laugh, glancing to see Dr. Kent's eyes dancing with amusement.

At seeing his enjoyment for the third time because of her rambling, her words finally ended. When would she ever learn to curb this horrible habit herself?

"I apologize," she mumbled. "I've let my tongue run away with me again."

"You needn't apologize."

"Do I not? Because each time I ramble on in such a way, you seem to find it unbearably amusing." She looked away. "As if I need a reminder that my behavior is not socially acceptable."

She couldn't count the number of times people had giggled behind their fingers or shared baffled expressions, all while they thought Lucy could not see. Aunt was always there to keep Lucy's tongue stilted and Mr. Carter, the same. Even her parents had done so on occasion, though usually only to make a good impression on various lords or ladies.

Yes, they'd all done their part to keep Lucy from embarrassing themselves and her. All of them...except Benjamin Kent.

Slowly, her eyes moved toward him. He stared at his hands laced together before him as he still leaned his elbows on his thighs, his fingers fiddling up and down. The candlelight flickered against the strong angle of his jawline, accentuating the facial hair he'd not had time to shave from his chin and jaw.

Her heart tickled inside her chest. "You have never stopped me."

"Beg your pardon?" He kept his gaze down.

"You have never stopped my rambling."

His fingers ceased their movement. "That is because I do not see the point in doing so. You will stop when you are ready to stop."

Was that true? She thought back to certain moments of her life when she had been allowed to speak as much as she wished to, and only then did she realize that Dr. Kent was absolutely right in his observation of her. She *did* eventually stop. How could she not have seen this herself?

Then another thought occurred. "May I ask why you laugh at me?"

"I do not laugh at you."

"Very well, you smile. But, why?"

His jaw twitched.

She waited impatiently. "If you haven't an answer for me, I shall simply assume the worst. You smile because you find it humorous to see me making a fool of myself."

He glanced at her sidelong. "That is not why."

"Well, I can think of no other reason. So unless you have anything else to say…"

She prayed her goading would work, relief rushing over her when it finally did.

He replied in a soft voice, his eyes averted. "I do not stop you because when you *ramble*, as you put it, you reveal more about yourself. And I…I enjoy learning more about you."

He leaned slightly toward her until their shoulders touched. Her skin responded with heated delight.

"And I smile," he continued, his voice low, "because your rambling is perhaps your most admirable trait. Excepting the way your eyes dance when you grin."

Lucy's breath caught in her throat when finally, his eyes found hers, their faces inches apart. "I've always enjoyed listening to you speak, Miss Lincoln. And I believe I always will."

She stared at him, heat flooding her cheeks as her heart beat fiercely against her chest. This man, how had she not seen him before? How had she not felt this physical attraction, this emotional attraction to him four years ago?

She was a fool, and apparently, she would *always* be a fool. For instead of thanking him for his kindness, she allowed her eyes to drift where they didn't belong.

His lips were slightly parted, as if inviting her to taste of them.

But she couldn't. It was late at night—*too* late. A member of her aunt's household could happen upon them at any moment. Lucy needed to see to Aunt Harriet. Dr. Kent needed to go home.

Yet still, Lucy peered at the man's mouth, an unforeseeable force pulling her closer. She wet her lips, tipping her head to the side, hesitating just a moment before closing the distance between them.

It was merely a soft brushing, the barest hint of a touch.

But Dr. Kent did not return it.

Any sensible woman would have pulled away, apologized for such shameless behavior. She was kissing the man whose proposal she rejected, for heaven's sake.

But if anything had been established that evening, it was that she was not a sensible woman.

She relished the feel of his warm lips on hers and wished to linger forever, but how could she when she was not certain if Dr. Kent wished to kiss *her*?

Slowly, she pulled back just enough to meet his gaze.

His eyes moved between hers, a guarded look in their green depths. Did he truly not wish to share in such affection? Had he not felt the same thing she had, the spark, the desire?

Or had she irreversibly extinguished that desire in him four years ago with her cruelty?

She waited as if an eternity, desiring only to return her lips to his, but she waited. And she waited. Until finally, his eyes drifted to a close, and he leaned toward her.

Instead of his lips remaining static on hers, they pressed into her with the warmth of a thousand suns. There was nothing urgent, nothing frantic or frenzied about his touch. It was soft and slow and pure.

And though she did not know how it would end, she knew she did not want it to.

For the first time in his life, Benjamin was glad to see his logic flee. How many years had he longed for this moment? How many years had he longed to feel Lucy's soft kiss on his lips?

When she'd first leaned forward, fear had frozen him. He wouldn't kiss her. He wouldn't be wooed by her talks of change and admiration of him.

And yet, her eyes had spoken the truth. Miss Lincoln felt something for him. And he needed to know exactly what.

He leaned in closer, breathing in the scent of her, memorizing the feel of her soft lips, her small nose just grazing his cheek as they shared in this affection he'd never thought possible.

He shifted toward her on the step they shared, sliding his right arm to encircle her back while his left hand reached toward her face.

Slowly, he caressed the soft skin of her cheek, and when she sighed, he was undone. He slipped his hand beneath her jaw, just as he'd done to check her pulse. With her quickened heartbeat beneath his fingertips, he secured his hold of her, tipping her head to the side to deepen their kiss, which she readily accepted.

She wanted to kiss him. He could feel it. As greatly as he wanted to kiss her.

And as he realized the truth in his thoughts, reality crushed down around him. All too swiftly, the memories of why he'd fallen for Miss Lincoln in the first place rushed back to him.

But he couldn't allow such a thing to happen. He couldn't allow those memories to lull him into a false sense of security, only to have her strip the very joy from his life once again.

Slowly, he pulled away, his hand longing to touch her face again the moment he released his hold of her. "I should go," he whispered.

She blinked, as if coming out of a daze. "Yes," she breathed. "And I should check on my aunt."

He pushed himself from the stairs and gathered his belongings. She made to follow him, but he softly shook his head. "I can see myself out." He needed to create distance between them. He needed to forget how enjoyable that kiss had been and how right it had felt.

"Thank you again for your help this evening," she said, crossing her arm in front of her chest and clasping the opposite shoulder.

"Of course. Do keep me informed of Mrs. Bird's health. And...and be sure to sleep yourself."

"I will."

With a deep breath, he gave a final nod then crossed the front hall to the door. Without bothering to don his outerwear, he slipped outside and closed the door behind him.

The freezing wind instantly gripped him in its clutches, and he released his pent-up breath.

This was just the thing to keep his mind away from the woman he'd left inside. The woman with whom he longed to return to and finish that kiss. But he wouldn't. Because that kiss had meant nothing to either of them.

Unless…unless she'd been sincere in her desire to change. Unless, somehow, her feelings for him had altered from four years ago.

If that was the case, then perhaps the kiss *had* meant something.

But what?

# CHAPTER 17

The next morning, when Aunt's eyes finally fluttered open, Lucy was at her bedside.

"Good morning," she whispered.

Aunt Harriet glanced around her, as if unsure of where she was before her eyes settled on Lucy. "My dear?" Her voice was hoarse, and she put a hand to her throat.

"Here." Lucy quickly leaned forward for a glass of water and helped her aunt to take a few sips.

"Thank you."

"Are you hungry? I can have Cook make a chicken broth for you."

She nodded, struggling to sit up, only to gasp when she put pressure on her right arm. Glancing down, she saw the bandage from where the surgeon had bled her. With parched lips, she grimaced. "You sent for Dr. Chelton then?"

Lucy remained silent for a moment. She had hoped the questions wouldn't start until much later. "I did. Just as you requested."

"Then my fever must have gotten worse."

"You don't recall what occurred?"

"The last I remember was speaking with you after the Callow's card party." Regret flashed across her face as she no doubt thought back to her harsh words spoken of Father.

But Lucy didn't wish to speak of such things. She propped a few pillows behind Aunt's back. "Your fever did get worse. Far worse."

Aunt's eyes watched her as Lucy moved across the room to open the curtains. "I thought for certain you would disregard my request and send for Dr. Kent."

Dr. Kent. The very name pulsed heat through her heart. Lucy had been entirely exhausted last night. Drained emotionally and physically. That was the reason she'd given herself for allowing that kiss to occur.

And yet, she still could not find it within her to regret their affection, even if she still did not know what it meant for their future. If it meant anything at all.

"I suppose Dr. Chelton deserves more credit than I give him," Aunt Harriet said, "if he was able to bring me back from such a fever."

Lucy clenched her fists against the curtains. She would not allow that poor excuse for a physician to take credit for Aunt's survival.

"Dr. Chelton does not deserve such praise, Aunt," she said softly, her back still turned away.

"Well, of course the surgeon does, too. And I'm certain you and Wright helped, as well, for which I cannot thank you enough."

Lucy flicked the curtains open just a sliver then slowly turned to face her. "You ought not be thanking us, either."

Aunt tipped her head to the side, the light revealing her gaunt expression—grey circles under her bloodshot eyes.

"It was Dr. Kent who saved your life."

Aunt's lips pressed together. "You brought him back."

"I did." Lucy stood with her back straight, unwilling to waver. "After Dr. Chelton's archaic practices placed you right at death's doorstep and it became clear you would not survive through the night, I sent for Dr. Kent." She raised her chin. "That man is the sole reason we speak now. He saved your life."

Aunt Harriet closed her eyes for a moment, drawing in a slow breath. "You love him. Don't you?"

That was certainly the last question Lucy had expected to have to answer. Love Dr. Kent? Of course not. Yes, she had kissed him, but did that mean she loved him?

"You needn't hide your feelings from me, Lucy," Aunt said, a heaviness hanging off the end of each word. "I can see it in your eyes when you speak of him—the respect, the admiration. Do not deny it."

Lucy looked away, her cheeks burning. Aunt had always encouraged Lucy's happiness, despite her forceful opinions over whom Lucy ought to marry. Perhaps if the truth was told, Aunt Harriet might be more accepting of whatever it was Lucy *did* feel for the gentleman.

She stepped toward the bed, taking the seat nearby with an averted gaze. "I cannot deny anything because I truly do not know how I feel anymore. Dr. Kent was always so timid. So silent. But now, he is confident and charming and sweet. I do admire him, but I don't know what else beyond that."

Her aunt leaned back against her pillows, closing her eyes. In a weakened voice, she said, "Thank heavens you haven't fallen in love with him yet."

Lucy's brow furrowed. She waited for more of an explanation, but Aunt's breathing had leveled. Had she fallen asleep again?

However, in the next moment, she spoke, her eyes still closed. "You know my opinion on marriage, Lucy. I respect your decision to one day find a spouse. But if I may be honest for a moment?" She didn't wait for permission before continuing. "Marriage to a man like Dr. Kent would destroy your life. It would make you change in unthinkable ways. I have seen the very same occur to others, and I would never forgive myself if I allowed the same to happen to you."

She fell silent once more, but thoughts jumbled so loudly within Lucy's mind, her head began to spin.

Aunt Harriet was speaking of Mother and Father's relationship. Lucy knew it. But then, how had Father in any way ruined Mama's life? They were both happy together. Lucy had never seen anything to tell her otherwise.

So why was Aunt so adamant that Papa had destroyed Mama, when Uncle Francis had been the true controlling gentleman?

"I suppose we really needn't be speaking of such things anyway," Aunt mumbled. "As you do not love him after all." She turned her head to the side opposite Lucy. "I think I'll sleep for a moment now, my dear. I fear my stamina is not what it was."

With a stomach clenched tighter than a rag wrung of all water, Lucy left the room. At least Aunt was correct in one regard. Lucy *wasn't* in love, so they didn't need to discuss such a thing.

Or did they?

Out of an abundance of caution, and because Aunt refused to see any other physician to ensure she was on the mend, Lucy remained at home with her for the next few days, bringing in the new year with only each other for company.

However, when the Gouldens' ball arrived, two days before Twelfth Night, Aunt assured Lucy she was more than well enough to attend.

"Sometimes I do wonder who is the elder in our relationship," Aunt joked as they reached the ball, Lucy having advised her to take care and not exert herself too greatly.

Lucy smiled. The feeling felt foreign to her lips. She and Aunt had kept their conversation cordial and conflict-free the past few days, though it was void of their usual carefree natures. She hadn't truly smiled since, well, since the night she'd kissed Dr. Kent.

Her heart jumped. She would be speaking with him tonight for the first time since then. She'd seen him passing by the townhome, striding down the street on the opposite side. His eyes had flickered toward the house, then he'd ducked his head and forged on.

She'd longed to see him and to speak with him. Especially after Aunt had asked Lucy if she loved him. She still couldn't say. But that evening she was hoping to finally receive the answer to the question herself.

Unfortunately, when they entered the Gouldens' ballroom and she spotted Dr. Kent, her conflicting feelings remained. She didn't know if she'd rather hide away in fear or run up to him with a broad smile and tell him just how greatly she'd missed seeing him these last few days.

What did that mean? Infatuation? Admiration? Love?

Her thoughts were a muddled mess until his eyes found hers, and a tentative smile spread across his lips as he headed in her direction.

Her heart stuttered so greatly, she could hardly draw in a breath.

"Stay strong, Lucy," Aunt whispered in her ear.

Stay strong? Stay strong against the gentle Benjamin Kent who would never hurt a soul? The Benjamin Kent who had saved both of their lives and no doubt countless others?

How on earth was Lucy to decipher what she was feeling with Aunt breathing down her neck every second of the evening?

"Mrs. Bird, Miss Lincoln," Dr. Kent said upon reaching them. "It's a pleasure to see you this evening."

"And you." Aunt's words were as stinted as her smile.

"It is good to see your health returned, Mrs. Bird."

Aunt swallowed what appeared to be a hearty dose of pride. "Yes, and I believe I have you to thank for it."

He gave a brief nod before turning his attention to Lucy. His smile appeared more genuine then. "Miss Lincoln, might you…might I request of you the first dance? Unless, of course, you are already occupied."

His eyes flitted away, his words falling softly, and Lucy smiled at his sudden discomfort. It reminded her of when they were younger.

"I would be happy to save my first for you, sir."

His smile returned, and he glanced awkwardly at Aunt before continuing. "I-I have something for you. I was going to bring it by the other day, but I thought this evening would be better."

Lucy's brow rose. "Something for me?"

He nodded. "I have to retrieve it. If you wouldn't mind waiting."

"No, of course not. I will wait right here for you."

He backed away with a nod of his head, his eyes dancing. "I shan't be but a moment."

Lucy bit her lip to hide her grin. What could he possibly have for her? And why did he seem nearly as excited as she was?

"Strange man," Aunt Harriet mumbled.

Lucy had all but forgotten Aunt standing at her side.

"I suppose it is wise of you to have the first dance with him," she continued. "That way you may overcome it in the beginning and look forward to the rest of the evening."

Lucy stifled a sigh. "Aunt, what—"

"Miss Lincoln! How marvelous you look this evening!"

She stopped her words as Mr. Carter appeared at her side. He took her hand in his and placed a kiss to the back of her glove.

Memories of their time together flickered through her mind. The Frost Fair. The ice breaking off. Dr. Kent saving her as Mr. Carter laughed elsewhere.

"Good evening, Mr. Carter," she greeted, forcing a smile as she put the thoughts from her mind. There was no need to begrudge him for simply behaving the way he always had.

His eyes scanned the length of her white gown and a red, sheer overlay. "My, but you look a portrait."

He'd said the very same to her and eyed her in the exact same way many times. But for some reason, this evening, his scrutiny made her shift away uneasily.

"And what of my own appearance, Mr. Carter," Aunt piped in, offering her hand to the gentleman next.

Mr. Carter grinned. "As beautiful as ever, madam."

He winked at Lucy. There was something off about his smile, his stare. But she couldn't put her finger on what it was.

"Are you looking forward to the evening, Mr. Carter?" Lucy asked next.

"Indeed. So long as the both of you agree to be my dance partners. For two different dances, of course."

Aunt laughed. When before Lucy would have jumped at the opportunity to dance with her friend, now, she merely smiled. Mr. Carter always made everything more fun. So why did her heart not flip with excitement at seeing him—when it did at seeing Dr. Kent?

Was it because she no longer trusted him? Was it because she feared he might abandon her in the middle of a dance as he'd abandoned her for Christmas dinner and then next upon the ice?

She glanced over his shoulder. When would Dr. Kent return? Could she excuse herself and wait elsewhere, away from Aunt and Mr. Carter?

"Are you well this evening, Miss Lincoln?" Mr. Carter asked.

She returned her attention to him. "Of course."

"Merely taken with my own beauty?" He flashed a smile, leaning closer to her. "Though, it fails in comparison to your own, of course."

The scent of strong drink singed her nose. Had he been drinking that much already? Perhaps that was why he seemed so…off.

"That must be it," she said.

His flirting usually made her giggle. But now, such words made her stomach tighten. Whether that was due to the alcohol on his breath or because she'd received real compliments from Dr. Kent, she couldn't be sure.

"Shall we dance the first, Miss Lincoln?"

"Thank you, but I have promised my first to Dr. Kent already."

His smile faltered. "Surely you can tell him I've already asked you."

She blinked. "Surely, I cannot."

To decline Dr. Kent now would be unthinkably cruel—not to mention improper. And that was to say nothing of the fact that she *wanted* to dance with him.

Mr. Carter chuckled tightly. "Since when have you ever given a care about being cruel to that man?"

Tension slipped between them—a tension that had never been there before. Just like with Aunt. "Why do you not dance the first with Aunt Harriet and the second with me?"

Mr. Carter shifted to Aunt Harriet. "A fine substitution, I daresay."

Aunt smiled, flattered. Before she could say a word, however, Mrs. Callow came up beside her.

"How delighted I am to see you've made a full recovery, my dear friend," the woman said.

As Aunt Harriet recounted her illness to a wide-eyed Mrs. Callow,

Mr. Carter moved to stand directly beside Lucy, the alcohol even stronger on his breath as he whispered down to her.

"Had I known you could not have said no to Benny Kent, I would've asked you for the first dance long ago, Miss Lincoln."

She took a deliberate step away from him. "I could have said no to him. But I didn't wish to."

Mr. Carter eyed her with disbelief. She knew what was coming next, the very same question Aunt had asked—did Lucy love Dr. Kent. But Lucy was not about to have such a conversation in such a place with Martin Carter.

Instead, she strapped on a smile and faced him directly. "At any rate, why is your first dance not already occupied?" She leaned in with a whisper. "With Miss Robins. I take it she is here this evening."

Had Lucy looked away for even a moment, she would have missed the dark cloud passing over his eyes before he grinned to replace it. "Why would I wish to dance with her more than you?"

Lucy narrowed her eyes. "Don't be daft."

He shrugged, looking away. "Yes, well. As women always are to me, she was simply a passing fancy." He turned back to face her. "All women but you, that is."

He flashed a smile, but Lucy hardly noticed. "How can that be so? The last time I saw you, there were veritable stars in your eyes as you spoke of her."

"Miss Lincoln, will you stop?" He slid a finger between his neck and cravat, lightly chuckling to force a flippant air, but Lucy knew better than to believe him. "There was nothing really between us. We enjoyed each other's company for a time then moved on, as I always do. Besides, nothing serious could have come about from our relationship anyway."

Lucy studied him as Dr. Kent so often studied her. His smile was clearly forced, and a flicker of pain, no, of sorrow, flashed in his eyes.

Her heart twisted with compassion. "She did not return your regard?" she whispered.

He raised a flippant shoulder. "Fortunately, my regard was not sincere."

Lucy did not believe him for a minute. She could not imagine his heartache. The first time he'd fallen for someone, and Miss Robins had not loved him in return.

"I'm so sorry," she said. "Can I help you in any way?"

"Dance the first with me?"

She sighed at his devilish grin. Heartbroken as he was, he was still Mr. Carter. "You know I cannot do that."

He reached for both of her hands, peering down at her. "Come now. You, dance with Dr. Kent? It hardly makes sense."

Alcohol once more drifted on the air toward her. Knowing what occurred between him and Miss Robins, now his drinking made sense that evening.

"But you and I," he continued, rubbing his thumbs on the back of her hands until they were raw with discomfort. "We make perfect sense."

She gently tried to pull away, but he held steadfast. She glanced to Aunt, who was still in deep conversation with Mrs. Callow. But others were sure to notice his lingering hold in the teeming ballroom. Others...such as Dr. Kent.

Firmly, she pulled her hands from his grip. "We make perfect sense for what, Mr. Carter? What are you trying to say?"

His gaze did not falter, a crazed look taking seed in his eyes. "I'm saying that we forget Miss Robins. That we forget Dr. Kent, and your aunt, and all else in the room. I'm saying that we dance the night away as we used to. Just the two of us. Dancing for far longer than is proper and creating rumors for all of London to share about us."

And have Dr. Kent assume she was attached to Mr. Carter? Never.

Clearly Mr. Carter's suggestion had been born of drink, for he would know how behaving in such a manner now, as they were no longer children and in London, of all places, her reputation would surely be ruined.

Still, she didn't wish to injure the man more than he already had been that evening. "I think it would be wise of us if we danced the customary one or two dances only, sir."

"Wise." He looked to the ceiling with a heavy sigh. "Being wise is far too glorified, surely. We ought to live life in the now with no thought for our future."

Wccks ago, Lucy would have joyfully agreed with his words. But now, his suggestion left her with a bad taste in her mouth, as if she'd just eaten burnt goose.

"Planning for the future is not so terrible," she said.

He stared at her, leaning slightly to the side before catching himself. "You are right. That is what we should be doing—planning for the future. *Our* future."

# CHAPTER 18

*L*ucy could have laughed, had not Mr. Carter's serious expression caused her stomach to churn. "You've had too much to drink tonight, Mr. Carter," she whispered. "You forget yourself *and* our lifelong friendship."

"Or perhaps that is the only thing I've not forgotten," he pressed on. "Just think of it. You would be giving your aunt precisely what she wants—a union between the two of us. And you would be mending my…my broken heart."

Why had he not admitted to it being broken until then? Was he trying to guilt her into accepting his proposal?

She glanced to Aunt, who was still unaware of anything occurring between them. "Mr. Carter, you are not thinking clearly."

"Oh, but I am!" His words slurred. "You have always been my dearest friend. What do you say? Shall we have a go of it?"

How wonderfully romantic. "Mr. Carter, I—"

The discordant sounds of violins behind them signaled the approach of the first dance, interrupting what Lucy had hoped to be a final denial of his drunken request.

"Mr. Carter?" Aunt's attention focused on them, her eyes settling on his hands still holding Lucy's. "Are you ready to have the dance of your life, sir?"

"I always am, Mrs. Bird." Mr. Carter released his hold of Lucy and offered his arm to Aunt Harriet instead. "Shall we?"

As he led her to the dance floor, Aunt gave Lucy a knowing look. Clearly, she still hoped for a union between her niece and Mr. Carter.

Lucy's stomach hardened. She could say just as assuredly now as she could before, such a thing would *never* occur.

"Miss Lincoln?"

Turning, she found Dr. Kent at her side.

"I do apologize for taking so very long," he said. "I...Are you well?"

She blinked, forcing aside what had just occurred and putting all her attention on the gentleman before her. "Yes, of course."

Of course he wouldn't believe her. He was far too observant for that. But mentioning Mr. Carter's proposal was the last thing she wished to do that evening.

"Shall we dance?" she asked.

He looked to where the other dancers were already gathering in the set. "Well, I..."

"Is something wrong?" Then she noted his hands clasped behind his back.

Of course. He'd gone to fetch something for her.

Despite herself, intrigue raised her spirits. "You were to show me something?"

He nodded, still averting his gaze. "If you do not mind missing a moment of the dance, I would prefer sharing this with you somewhere a little...quieter."

Lucy was more than happy to oblige, leading the way to a corridor outside of the main ballroom. People filtered in and out, though the noise was far less away from the dancers.

When they reached an outer window, Lucy faced him. "Will this suffice?"

He nodded, his lips in a taut line. "Forgive me for the hassle."

"It is no trouble," she said, anxiously glancing to his hands still held behind his back. "Although, if you make me wait a moment longer to see what you have hidden behind your hands, I might die of curiosity."

A smile flickered across his features. "I shall keep you in suspense no longer then." With unassuming movements, Dr. Kent pulled his hands out before her, revealing a brown, leather-bound book.

Lucy tipped her head to the side. "What is this?"

He offered it to her, and her heart skipped. She took the book, turning it to the side to see the spine. Near the top, she read the words aloud. "*The Life of Nelson*, by Robert Southey." Her lips parted. "You found it?"

He nodded, a smile fighting its way across his lips.

She ran her fingers across the cover then opened the book. A portrait of Admiral Nelson's profile was printed on the left side, and on the right, the title was written with the name of the author beneath it. "How?" she breathed. "We've been to Barrington Books, Hatchards, and countless other bookshops. No one possessed it."

"I must confess, this is a used copy. I've had it in my personal library for a year now, though I've only read it once."

"Oh, I thought...Here." She handed the book back to him, embarrassment creeping up her neck and settling as a deep heat in her cheeks. "My apologies for the assumption. I thought you were giving it to me to give to my father, but that was rather ridiculous of me to assume. How terribly silly of me." She glanced over her shoulder, ready to flee from her mistake. "Would you like to join the dance before it ends? Or would you prefer a refreshment instead? Or if you'd rather go elsewhere with someone other than me, of course I would understand. I..."

Once again, her words ended as his smile began. But as she recalled his kind words the evening before about her rambling, her embarrassment settled, if only by a small degree.

"Miss Lincoln," he said softly, "the book is for you. Well, for you to give to your father. From what you've said, I believe he would appreciate it more than I do now."

The warmth fanned within her, a growing flame of peace and joy.

"But how can I take what is yours? Surely you will allow me to pay for it."

But he firmly shook his head. "No, I do not need compensation. And you are not taking it, I am giving it to you. I am only sorry I brought it to the ball, as I didn't think I would be welcome at your aunt's home after..." He trailed off with a shake of his head. "At any rate, I couldn't wait a day longer, as I know you are expecting the arrival of your parents soon. But...it has only now just occurred to me you have nowhere to put it."

His cheeks tinged a slight pink, and Lucy's heart felt full to bursting. How could she have ever thought this man to be dull or ordinary? How could she have ever felt indifferently toward him?

A strange sort of discomfort welled within her as her thoughts continued. A pleasant discomfort, like the feeling that occurred right before jumping across a creek or before sailing over a hedge on a horse. It was exhilarating and frightening at the same time.

But, oh, how she welcomed it.

She smoothed a hand across the book once more. "You needn't worry, Dr. Kent. I shall simply tuck it away with my cloak. It was very thoughtful of you to bring it tonight and so very kind of you to give it to me. My father will be so pleased."

"And you...are you pleased?"

Her heart knocked against her chest, as if begging to be released, to explore her true feelings. So that is exactly what she did.

"I've never been so pleased," she answered. "I've never been so happy."

Would he understand her meaning? Read the feeling behind her words?

His green eyes studied her, as if determining what she was saying was true. She couldn't blame him for his hesitation, but if she could convince him that she *had* changed, that her feelings for him had changed, perhaps they could be...

Loud cheering from the ballroom ended her thoughts, signaling the completion of the dance.

He turned to her with an apologetic look. "I'm sorry to have kept you away from dancing."

"It is no matter. After all, there are plenty of other dances to be had. If you would not mind asking me for another, that is."

Finally, a smile broke across his lips, and like the sun spreading its warmth across a frozen field of snow, Lucy's heart melted.

"In that case, Miss Lincoln, might I ask—"

"Benny, what are you doing at a ball?"

Lucy's stomach dropped. Of all times, why—*why*—did Mr. Carter choose to appear now?

He clasped Dr. Kent on the shoulder, sending a smirk toward Lucy. "I didn't see you on the dance floor, Miss Lincoln. Did Benny here lead you to the wrong room?"

Dr. Kent's jaw flexed as he stepped to the side, Mr. Carter's arm falling from Dr. Kent's shoulder.

"Dr. Kent and I were simply speaking and lost track of time," she said.

Mr. Carter barked out a laugh. Had he somehow managed another drink between ending the dance and finding Lucy? And where had he left Aunt Harriet?

She glanced over his shoulder as Mr. Carter motioned to the novel in her hands. "What in heaven's name are you doing with that at a ball?"

She brought the book close to her chest, cradling it near her heart. "It was a gift. From Dr. Kent." She tried to share a smile with the physician, but he averted his hardened gaze.

Mr. Carter laughed again. "Ah, now that explains it. Put it to the bookish physician to bring such an item to a ball. I'm surprised you're not reading it now, sir, in the back corners of the room as you used to."

Mr. Carter glanced to Lucy, no doubt to see if she cracked a smile. Perhaps years ago, her thoughtless self would have. But now, now she found his jokes distasteful and cruel.

Dr. Kent hardly seemed affected at all, though. He remained stoic, his eyes unmoving from Mr. Carter.

Mr. Carter, in turn, reduced his chuckling to an awkward huff then looked away, taking an inadvertent step back.

Lucy could not believe what she was seeing. She'd always wondered why Dr. Kent had not stood up for himself more. He was taller and broader in stature than Mr. Carter, yet Dr. Kent had never used such to his advantage, only ever walking away from conflict in silence.

But now, observing the same thing occurring again, Lucy realized...Dr. Kent did not have to resort to fists and criticisms. With a mere stare, he'd done the job.

Mr. Carter may have been filled with joy and passion for life and adventure. But Dr. Kent was mature, calm, and collected. He was filled with selfless service and a passion for helping others.

What could be more admirable than that?

Mr. Carter cleared his throat, his smile gone. "Shall we make our way to the dance floor, Miss Lincoln?"

Blast. She'd forgotten she'd promised the second to him.

He offered her his arm, but she glanced to Dr. Kent anxiously. "We still have a few moments left before it begins, I'm sure."

Mr. Carter frowned. "Yes, but I should very much like to finish our conversation from before."

Her insides twisted. She did not wish to continue that conversation. Not in the slightest. Not ever. But Mr. Carter was as headstrong as she was, and if he wished to continue the conversation, he would push for it until he received what he desired, regardless of how she felt.

"Perhaps we may speak of such things another time," she said softly.

Mr. Carter took a subtle step toward her, but her eyes were on Dr. Kent, who remained as silent and pensive as ever.

Mr. Carter must have noticed her lingering gaze on the physician, for he shifted his attention to him, too. "There are quite a few pretty women here this evening, are there not, Dr. Kent?"

Lucy narrowed her eyes. What was he about?

"There are always a number of fine women, Mr. Carter," Dr. Kent said, speaking for the first time. "One must learn to see the merit below one's skin, though."

Could Lucy fall for him even more?

Mr. Carter nodded, his eyes wide. "Oh, indeed, sir. Indeed. I see a number of girls who have a great deal of merit, as well as beauty. In fact..." He looked to Lucy. "I might be persuaded to finally marry because of someone in attendance here this very evening."

Both men stared at her, and she froze.

Lucy was not unaware of the similarities between what was occurring now and what had occurred four years ago—a ball, an unwanted proposal, an audience. The only thing different was the gentleman asking. And the fact that she was in love with someone else.

As certain as she was that Mr. Carter's proposal had been born from drink, she could not be cruel to him as she was cruel to Dr. Kent. But what could be said?

The voices around her grew louder as the side room filled with more guests. She knew Aunt would find her soon and press her opinion on Lucy, as well.

With a knot in her stomach, her discomfort grew, and then the inevitable words began.

"There *are* a number of pretty girls here," she said. "And I believe it is good to find merit beneath one's skin. I do the very same for men. I'm sure most women do. Of course, my aunt does not." She gave an uncomfortable laugh. "But I'm sure most of Society knows she doesn't wish to ever marry again. She does have a valid argument, though. She had a terrible marriage, and now she chooses to remain single. I wonder if I might do the very same, because—"

"Miss Lincoln," Mr. Carter interrupted with a wary glance around him, as if fearing someone had heard her incessant words and would judge *him* for it. "Are you well?"

He'd stopped her. Just like everyone did.

Everyone but Dr. Kent. She glanced to the physician, and her heart fell to the floor. His eyes had hardened, but they could not mask the pain hidden in their green depths.

Her words echoed in her mind. *"...Aunt chooses to remain single. I wonder if I might do the very same..."*

Dr. Kent must have thought her words were meant for him, not for Mr. Carter. How could she have been so stupid?

He took a step back, placing a hard smile on his lips. "Excuse me. I must find my partner for the next dance." He nodded without a glance at Mr. Carter then stepped away.

"Dr. Kent, wait, please."

He looked over his shoulder at her, though he continued walking ahead. "Good day, Miss Lincoln. I do hope your father enjoys the book."

Lucy stared helplessly at his retreating figure. What could she say to bring him back?

"Come, Miss Lincoln. Rid yourself of that ridiculous book and then let us dance all night together."

Anger boiled within her. She turned on Mr. Carter, scowling. "This book is not ridiculous, Mr. Carter, you are." She pressed a finger into his chest, speaking through clenched teeth. "How dare you? How dare you criticize Dr. Kent and me? How dare you propose to me while clearly having had far too much to drink!"

A few people glanced with wide eyes, but she hardly cared. Mr. Carter stood back, stunned. "Miss Lincoln, I—"

"No, we are finished, Mr. Carter. In response to your preposterous proposal, I give a very firm and resounding no. You are heartbroken over your Miss Robins. You love her, not me. To pretend otherwise is unjust to the both of us."

He ducked his head, evidence that she'd been right about his proposal all along.

"Now, you either go home this moment or swear to me that you will not speak to another young woman tonight in the chance that you injure her as you have just injured me and Dr. Kent."

His lips pulled down, but he nodded all the same. "Yes, ma'am."

Feeling as if she'd just scolded a toddler, Lucy drew in a deep, calming breath. The man was wounded, after all. Just like she was. "I hope we may move past this as friends, Mr. Carter. And I pray that you may one day find a woman deserving of your love. But you and I both know that woman is not I. Goodnight, sir."

With a firm nod, she stepped away from him, clutching her book to her chest in search of Dr. Kent, but when Aunt found her moments later, she knew all hope was lost.

"Heavens, Lucy, what has happened? You're as red as your gown."

"Nothing at all. Tell me, have you seen Dr. Kent?"

Aunt's lips tightened. "I believe I saw him darting out of the door only a moment a go with his coat and hat."

Lucy closed her eyes. She'd lost her chance. "I think I should like to go home now, Aunt."

In a few moments, they sat facing each other in the carriage, Lucy's eyes fixed on the window that lit with every passing lamp, each one a brief flicker of hope before darkness reminded her of her own reality.

"Lucy?" Aunt's soft voice drifted toward her from across the carriage seat.

"Yes?"

"Might you tell me what has occurred this evening to have made you wish to leave early?"

Lucy had little desire to go into such details, but then, wouldn't alerting Aunt of her true feelings, telling her of Mr. Carter's tactless proposal, help her to see her side?

She drew in a deep breath. "Mr. Carter proposed to me."

Aunt gasped, biting her lip to keep from smiling, though her eyes still sparkled. "Did he?"

"Before you are too overcome with excitement, you must know that I declined his offer."

Aunt blinked several times, as if unable to comprehend the decision.

Well, Lucy would do her best to inform her of the truth. "He was drunk, Aunt."

"Are you certain?"

"Yes," she answered firmly. "You danced with him. Surely you smelt it on him."

"I suppose there was a distinct whiff a time or two."

Lucy sighed at Aunt's denial. "Even if he'd had his wits about him, Mr. Carter had just had his heart broken by another woman. His offer was not of the serious nature."

Aunt looked away, her brow pulled together with disappointment.

"I must tell you," Lucy continued, "that even if his offer had been in earnest, my answer would have still been no."

Aunt Harriet sat by in silence, the light they rode by sliding across her face and illuminating her serious expression.

Lucy struggled to maintain her courage. She did not know if Aunt would accept her words any more than Lucy did not know if Dr. Kent would accept *Lucy* after all they'd been through. But she had to try, and she had to be honest.

"I finally have an answer to your question, Aunt. I know you will not approve, but after this evening, I can no longer deny it. I love—"

"Stop." Aunt closed her eyes, wincing. "Please, don't. I cannot bear to hear such an admission."

Lucy shook her head in disbelief. Never had Aunt been so unmanageable. "Why can I not speak the truth?"

"Because I cannot bear to hear it. I cannot bear to see you throw your life away."

Lucy squared her shoulders. She would get to the bottom of Aunt Harriet's qualms if it was the last thing she did.

"Is that why you did not tell me the real reason you wished to go to the bookshop?" she asked. "Because you believe you would be throwing away your own life if you voiced aloud your attraction to Mr. Barrington?"

In the brief light, the tendons of Aunt's neck protruded. "Mr. Barrington?"

Her words only proved the fact that Lucy was correct in her assumption. "Aunt, you've never once enjoyed going in bookshops before."

She raised both eyebrows, smiling in an attempt to lighten the air between them, but Aunt merely glanced away with discomfort.

"Well, such a thing hardly matters now. I shan't go back there, as you've already been given the book you've been searching for."

She motioned to the book Lucy still grasped on her lap. All thanks to the wonderful Dr. Kent.

"Forgive me," Lucy said, "but I don't believe that is the real reason you will not be going back there."

Aunt raised her chin.

"Something happened between the two of you. You can deny it all you wish, but I saw the ruddiness of your cheeks and the swift way in which you left his shop just before you fell ill."

Aunt's cheeks reddened. "Very well. I do not know why you must press me for such information, as it hardly matters. The man proposed, and I declined. That is all there is to it."

Lucy's conscience twisted. How many hearts would the two of them break by their refusals? Aunt Harriet clearly held a certain affection for the man. Would she truly keep herself from being happy based on what happened in the past?

"Why did you decline?" she asked.

Aunt scoffed. "Because he is a bookshop owner, and I am a lady. It would have never worked between the two of us. And yes, I would have surely thrown my life away with any other decision."

Lucy paused, vetting through response after response. She would think logically and rationally about this. Then their conversation would end amicably, and all would be well.

Or so, at least, she hoped.

"And you believe your marrying Mr. Barrington—and my falling in love with Dr. Kent—would be ending our lives because of your own relationship with Uncle Francis or because of my parents' relationship?"

"Both."

Lucy shook her head. "How can you even compare the two? You were not happy with Uncle Francis, but my parents *are* happy."

Aunt looked away, her words muffled. "Yes, only because your mother changed herself to please your father."

The words tossed viciously in Lucy's stomach like snow kicked up from a horse's hooves. But she would not believe them. "Aunt…"

"Your mother and I were inseparable as children, Lucy," Aunt

Harriet began before Lucy could say another word. "We were the very same in every regard. Full of life. Free as we wished to be. We grew up chasing our dreams and running wild." Her eyes hardened. "Then your father came along and forced her to become as dull as he is."

Lucy frowned. "Just because he lives life differently than you does not make him dull."

Aunt peered over at her, a sorrowful smile across her lips. "You sound just like your mother. I will be forever grateful that your father makes my sister as happy as she claims to be. But that does not mean I do not long for her true self to one day return, despite Mr. Lincoln's wishes."

The very idea of Papa forcing anyone to do anything they did not wish to do was simply preposterous. His servants, indeed, all of Fawsley, respected him. Mama and Lucy loved him. He had always encouraged his daughter to choose her own spouse and supported his wife in whatever she wished.

With all of this true, how could Aunt be so misinformed? Did she simply allow her marriage with Uncle Francis to taint reality?

"May I ask, Aunt, what made you marry Uncle Francis?"

"Duty," Aunt replied in a flattened tone. "Unfortunately, I made a poor decision, just like my sister."

Lucy's chest tightened at yet another slight to her father. Clearly, Aunt Harriet now believed the lies she'd fed herself about Papa, merely because she was bitter for losing her sister.

But then, if she believed those things about Father, was what she said about her own husband false, too? Lucy had only been seven when they'd married, fifteen when he'd died. Could Aunt have been feeding lies about Uncle Francis to Lucy all along?

And if that was the truth, how could Lucy believe anything Aunt Harriet said?

"I only wish you could see the true intents of my heart, Lucy," Aunt whispered, breaking through the silence. "I merely offer you my sage advice, my help, to keep you from making a poor decision you will one day regret."

She leaned forward, grasping Lucy's hand in her cold gloves as they rested atop the warm book in Lucy's lap. "Watching you grow into the woman you are now, a woman so like *me*, has been the greatest joy of my life. You kept me alive during my marriage, and you are keeping me alive now. To lose you at this time would be unbearable."

Lucy opened her mouth to protest, but Aunt shook her head and continued. "I rue the day I allowed that physician into my home. Had I known you would not have been sensible and strong enough to withstand his wiles..." She broke off, sighing with a pleading look in her eye. "Please, my dear. I cannot see you throw your life away as your mother did. I cannot lose my Lucy."

The carriage rolled to a stop in front of the townhome, and Lucy pulled her hands away. Her stomach tossed, but it was not due to the motion of the carriage. Aunt's words had sickened her. She was not selfless in her desire to see Lucy happily married. She wished to keep her niece as a pet. A doll. A mere object to help pass the time in her lonely, abject life.

Never mind what Lucy wished for. Never mind that she had never felt more at peace with who she was becoming. Aunt cared far more about her own feelings than Lucy's.

And Lucy felt betrayed.

"My dear?" Aunt asked as the carriage door was opened.

Tears billowed in Lucy's eyes. "I...I need to be alone, Aunt Harriet. Excuse me."

With swift movements, she left the carriage, scurrying up the stairs and into the house without a glance back.

She'd been intent on fleeing to her room for the foreseeable future, but when soft voices sounded from the parlor, she halted. Was that...

She retraced her steps until she stood in the door of the parlor. There, seated together on the couch with smiles on their faces as they spoke with one another, sat her parents.

"Mama? Papa?"

They turned at once at the sound of their daughter's voice and stood to greet her with bright expressions.

Lucy's tears flowed freely from her eyes then as she ran toward them, returning their embrace as she sent a silent prayer of gratitude heavenward that they arrived at the precise moment she needed them most.

# CHAPTER 19

*B*enjamin didn't bother stifling his yawn as he left another one of his patient's homes. The day had been filled with visit after visit of one sick person to the next. Colds, aches, fevers, wounds from falling.

He'd had another visit with Lady Sanders's daughter, Lady Anne, who'd slipped on a slab of ice on the steps of Clarendon Hotel. Fortunately, she was on the mend already, recovering as swiftly as…

No, he wasn't thinking of Miss Lincoln any longer.

With a heavy sigh, he removed his hat for a moment and raked his gloved fingers through his hair.

It was getting warmer, but only slightly. At least the majority of people weren't at the Frost Fair any longer. He couldn't bear the injuries that continually came from there. Those who visited the fair were foolish. Just like Miss Lincoln and her aunt. Just like he was.

He tried to force aside his thoughts once again but to no avail. They rained down upon him like a summer storm, swift and cold. Unable to be stopped.

He'd entirely lost his logic since first seeing Miss Lincoln at the fair. He'd behaved ridiculously, kissing her in the middle of the night, spending all hours of the day thinking of her, hoping that perhaps she might have changed, that she might have feelings for him.

But his biggest regret of all? Allowing himself to hope that perhaps *he* should renew his feelings for *her*.

He'd given her one of his favorite books for that very reason. She'd seemed to be more than receptive, until she'd set him aside with her comments about remaining single. At first, he'd hoped that perhaps she'd said such words for Mr. Carter's benefit, but everyone knew that man would never marry.

And Benjamin was made the fool again.

Miss Parfitt would've made better use of his time, but Benjamin had burned that bridge already, as he'd seen the girl on Mr. Lampton's arm twice since Benjamin had left the Callows' card party early.

Clenching his fists together, Benjamin forced his thoughts to the present. Dwelling on Mr. Carter or Miss Lincoln or even Miss Parfitt was no longer worth the effort.

Thank heavens he hadn't become too attached to Miss Lincoln for him to be so gravely injured again.

Yet, even as he thought the words, his heart twinged with that same ache he'd felt four years before, when Lucy Lincoln had broken his heart.

For she had just done it again.

Lucy had missed this. Sitting in the drawing room after dinner, visiting with her parents. Fire blazing in the hearth and bellies filled with hearty food.

She'd been relieved when Aunt had retired early that evening, leaving Lucy and her parents to themselves. The tension between her and Aunt Harriet had yet to fade since their argument, and having her there while Lucy gifted Father the book from Dr. Kent would have only deepened the wound.

"This really is marvelous, Lucy," Papa said, bringing her attention back to the drawing room as he thumbed through the pages of his new book, wonder filling his eyes like a boy eying his new horse.

The three of them typically exchanged gifts on Twelfth Night, but Lucy had been unable to keep the gift to herself any longer. "I'm so glad you like it, Father."

Mama smiled dotingly between the both of them, quietly sitting beside Lucy with a contented look.

"Did you purchase it here in Town?" Father asked.

All at once, Lucy's heart wilted like a rose after the first frost. "I was planning to, but I could not find it anywhere. A friend of mine had one in his possession that he graciously delivered to me, knowing I was in search of one."

"A friend?" Mama asked. "Anyone we might know?"

Lucy had yet to mention a word of Dr. Kent to her parents. They'd always respected the Kents of Fawsley but voicing aloud everything that had occurred between her and Dr. Kent seemed too painful, especially after what had happened with Aunt. But she could no longer put off the inevitable.

"Yes, you will know him. It was Dr. Kent."

Papa finally glanced up from his book. "Kent? The apothecary's son?"

"Indeed."

"How kind of him. Though that does not surprise me, considering his good family. I shall have to thank him when next I see him." Papa moved back to the book, gently sifting from page to page.

But Mama still watched Lucy. "Dr. Kent," she mused. "I have not seen him for years."

"Nor had I," Lucy said.

"Was this the first time you've seen him since his proposal?"

Lucy swallowed. "It was."

Mama watched her expectantly. "And…was it uncomfortable?"

Before Lucy knew it, a laugh escaped her lips. "More uncomfortable than you can imagine. He was the physician who tended to me after I fell on the ice at the Frost Fair."

Papa's eyes darted up again. "The Frost Fair?"

Mama frowned. "You fell on the ice?"

"Your aunt no doubt encouraged you to go," Papa mumbled softly. "It's a wonder you survived the last few weeks alone with her."

As much as Lucy wished for Aunt Harriet to receive the brunt of the blame, she couldn't lie. "I was more adamant that we see the Frost Fair than Aunt was. And I assure you, she was exceedingly careful afterwards. She took great care of me."

A sadness rushed over Lucy. Aunt always *had* taken great care of Lucy. She'd always seemed to want the best for her niece. So why could she not accept that Lucy had fallen in love with a physician?

"What is it, my dear?" Mama reached over, placing a hand over Lucy's. "You seem troubled."

The words perched at the edge of Lucy's tongue. Could she dare share her feelings after Aunt had criticized Mama and Papa, and then proceeded to critique Lucy's own heart?

As Mama watched her with a softened gaze and Papa lowered his book, Lucy knew at once that she could. Her parents would listen to her, and they would never injure her. With a deep breath, she began. "I am in love with Dr. Kent."

Mama's mouth opened, her eyes bright. "Heavens."

"Heavens, indeed," Papa said as his brow rose.

Lucy winced. "I am sorry to deliver such shocking news to the both of you, especially without any notice. But it is the truth."

Her parents remained silent for a moment, exchanging glances before turning to face Lucy again.

Mama blinked, clearly attempting to hide her surprise. "Well, that is shocking news, indeed. How...how did it come about?"

Lucy shrugged. "I cannot tell you. I only know that my eyes have been opened to the sort of man he truly is. If everyone knew the real Benjamin Kent as I now do—the thoughtful, intelligent gentleman that he is—they would not be able to keep themselves from falling in love with him, either."

"Oh, my dear," Mama said, tears glistening in her eyes. "This is wonderful news."

Though she'd expected such a reaction from her ever-gracious mother, Lucy was still overcome with relief. But all too soon, her heart sunk back deep into the cavity of her aching chest.

"It *would* be wonderful," she said, "if only I knew if he could still love me in return. I caused him a great deal of pain all those years ago, and I doubt very much that he'd wish to risk his heart again."

Mama tightened her grip around Lucy's hand. "Have you spoken to him at all about your feelings? Does he know how you feel now?"

"No. There have been moments, but nothing vocal."

"Then perhaps you ought to be speaking with him right now instead of the two of us," Mama suggested with a warm smile. "You ought not be sorrowful unless you know for certain he will not have you."

Lucy's heart leapt to her throat. Tell Dr. Kent how she felt? "I...I do not know if I can. I am far too fearful of rejection." Tears brimmed at the edge of her eyes. "For that is truthfully what I deserve."

Papa's chair creaked against the floor as he leaned forward. He still clasped the book between his hands, though his attention focused fully on his daughter. "You cannot keep holding on to the regrets of your past, Lucy, dear. Especially since you have changed for the better. You must learn to move forward, to forgive yourself." He paused, a smile tugging at his lips. "I assure you, if Dr. Kent still feels an ounce of what he felt for you before, one word about your own feelings will render him completely unable to refuse you."

Hope flapped within her like a bird attempting to take its first flight. "You...you are sure?"

Papa leaned back with a shrug. "I only have personal experience as evidence. The moment your mother said she loved me, I never looked back. I was finally convinced to marry her."

Mama scoffed, though her eyes held a playful light. "Please, Mr. Lincoln. You were begging me to marry you from the beginning."

Father winked, and Mama shook her head with a broad smile.

With their happy interaction, another worry was pulled in to snuff out the light that struggled so hard to brighten Lucy's mood.

"Perhaps you are right," she said with a wary nod. "I ought to speak with him. But there is another matter that must be resolved first." She glanced between her parents. "Aunt Harriet..."

Lucy thought she would have had to explain more, but her parents locked eyes and sighed in unison.

"We were afraid of this," Mama said as Father's lips slipped into a rigid line.

"Afraid of what?" Lucy asked.

Mama softened her tone. "That your aunt's rather overbearing opinions might keep you from your happiness, as they almost did mine."

Lucy stared. "What?"

Papa opened his book, his nostrils flaring. "Harriet did her very best to try to convince your mother not to marry me. I was far too dreary a gentleman for either one of them, you see."

"For her," Mama corrected. "You've never been dull in my eyes."

Lucy's heart swirled with warmth. Deep down, she'd known the truth between her parents, but Aunt's words had unsettled her, disrupting the peaceful environment she'd always felt when around her parents.

"Aunt Harriet told me Papa would not marry someone as reckless as you were, so he forced you to change."

Mama laughed mirthlessly. "Goodness. Harriet was never one to keep her opinion to herself, was she? No matter what falsehoods are spread in the process." She faced Lucy with another shake of her head. "That is not what occurred. It is true that I was once as carefree and spontaneous as she was, but I outgrew such behavior long before I met your father. Your aunt merely pretends it coincided precisely with when I met him."

Understanding flooded Lucy's mind. Now it all made sense. "And was Uncle Francis as terrible as Aunt made him out to be?"

Mama tipped her head back and forth, as if weighing her words. "That is difficult to say. He was a hard gentleman, certainly not as loving as your father. But I believe he truly did love Harriet, in his own way. She simply could not bear an ounce of restriction—and marriage, for her, was a restriction. That is why it is so important to choose one's spouse carefully. Thankfully, I did just that."

They both glanced to Father, who chewed on his lower lip. Was he attempting to keep quiet? Did he disapprove of Aunt Harriet as greatly as she disapproved of him?

Mama sighed. "My sister was not always so opinionated—"

Father coughed, though he said nothing else, and Mama hid her smile. "Very well, she was always opinionated. But since Mr. Bird's death, she's become unbearable. I assume she has taken the responsibility to ensure you marry someone who will not ruin your life, as marrying your father has supposedly ruined mine?"

Lucy grimaced. "Yes. Martin Carter, to be exact."

Father sat forward. "Martin Carter? That man is worse than..." He stopped at Mama's pointed look. "He is-is perfectly fine, if you like the man, of course."

Lucy laughed. "Worry not, Papa. I feel no love for him."

His shoulders lowered in relief.

"Has Harriet been forcing the two of you together?" Mama asked.

Lucy nodded. "As much as possible. She believes he is the perfect match for me." She shook her head. "He may be carefree, but he's too selfish for me to have ever considered him a spouse. That is exactly what Aunt disapproves of in Dr. Kent, though. She believes him to be far too level-headed and calm."

"Far too much like me," Father stated without a hint of malice.

Lucy had already determined to keep to herself Aunt's cruel opinion of Father, but apparently, he was already aware of it.

Slowly, she nodded. "That is one of her qualms, yes. She also does not approve of his upbringing, being the son of an apothecary."

"And do you care about that?" Mama asked carefully.

Lucy frowned. "Of course not. Not in the slightest. Should we marry," she paused, a blush creeping up her cheeks, "we would live comfortably, I'm certain. He's ambitious and has already made a good name for himself here. Though, he's talked of opening a practice by the sea."

Papa's brow raised with intrigue, and Lucy nearly smiled, had Aunt Harriet's words not been pressing on her conscience.

Silence filled the air between them until Mama proceeded with a gentle tone. "My dear, your father and I have done our best to raise you to be a confident young woman. We wish you to marry who you desire, not who your aunt desires."

"And we want you to make the decision yourself," Papa added in, "regardless of our own feelings."

Mama nodded in agreement.

The clouds parted above Lucy's spirits. "So on the rarity that Dr. Kent would have me, that he would open his heart up to me again… neither of you would disapprove of my marrying the physician?"

Mama tipped her head, her smile warm. "How could I ever disapprove of someone who clearly makes my daughter as happy as my husband has made me?" She stared at Father then, who watched her with as much admiration as Mama had for him. "I am a better woman because of him, and I would not change that for the world."

Lucy's heart soared, the fire from the hearth seeming to have leapt right into her chest. "That is just how I feel about Dr. Kent. He's helped me to see the ways I can change, but still accepts me for who I am. I love him more than anything." She met her parents' smiling faces with her own. "And I know what I wish to do now. Only…Aunt will heartily disapprove."

"All the better to do it then," Papa mumbled, pulling on an innocent expression when Mama shook her head disapprovingly. "What did I say?"

He winked at Lucy, who grinned. "In that case," she said, "I wonder, might the two of you help me with something?"

# CHAPTER 20

*B*enjamin rapped the door knocker of Mrs. Bird's townhome, wondering what the devil had convinced him to respond to the letter he'd just received.

A guilty conscience, that's what it was. He could never turn away a sick soul, especially when the rest of his day was free of other appointments.

He clasped his hands behind his back with his bag, fiddling his fingers against the handles as he once more recounted the letter he'd received only an hour before.

*Dr. Kent,*

*I'm certain this note will come as a surprise to you, as we haven't spoken in many years. But I've heard word that you are as excellent as a physician as one comes, and I'm afraid that I am in need of said excellent physician.*

*You see, on my journey to London with Mrs. Lincoln, I fear I became overly exhausted with our travels. As such, I've been excessively achy in my joints. I'd appreciate you coming to see an aging man to help in his ailments at your earliest convenience. As we do not typically come to Town, we have no one else to turn to, but I have no qualms whatsoever entrusting my care to you.*

*Do send word the moment you may come.*

*My deepest gratitude,*
*Mr. B. Lincoln.*

Benjamin had instantly written a refusal with the excuse of being too busy. Next, he'd scribbled out a note for the apothecary to have a tonic made for the man.

Then his conscience had gotten the better of him.

And now, he stood at the door of the woman he'd vowed to never speak with again.

At least he knew Mrs. Bird would be doing her best to keep Miss Lincoln away from him. That is, if Miss Lincoln wasn't doing so herself. She surely would never wish to see Benjamin again, and that was more than fine with him.

When the butler answered the door, Benjamin was shown into the empty parlor, and he waited for Mr. Lincoln to arrive, wandering to the window and absentmindedly staring at the snow-covered trees. The last time he'd been inside that townhome, he and Miss Lincoln had shared a k—

The door clicked open. Thank heavens Mr. Lincoln was there to end Benjamin's reckless thoughts.

Only, Mr. Lincoln had not entered the room.

"Miss Lincoln?"

His heart thumped painfully against his chest as the woman slowly closed the door behind her. All the while, her eyes focused on him.

What was she doing in there with her blonde hair swept up into elegant curls, white day dress gracefully draping down her body?

"Good morning, Dr. Kent," she said, her voice as smooth as always as she clasped her hands before her.

He looked away, clearing his throat. "I was told to meet your father here." He'd hate for her to think he was calling on her.

"I know." She took a few steps forward, her pink slippers poking out at the toes. "I asked him to write to you, as I didn't think you would come should I send for you myself."

She was certainly right about that. He had a mind to leave right then and there for her trickery. But his blasted conscience stopped him once again.

"Perhaps you ought to tell me what ails you then," he said, "should you even have an ailment, of course."

Surely that was the only reason she would send for a physician.

"I do." She swallowed. "I have an ache of the heart."

His brow twitched. What was she saying, that she was having chest pains? Trouble breathing? He took a quick scan of her face and body. She was not doubled over, nor did she appear to have any difficulty breathing.

Her eyes, however, were filled with pain.

Finally, her words sunk into his mind, though he stopped them before they could reach his heart. He would not allow this woman to press hope into his soul when she would simply thieve it right back.

He clasped his bag and clenched his jaw. "I fear I cannot help you with that."

She blinked, clearly startled with the harshness of his tone.

He looked away again, if only to avoid feeling the guilt her wide eyes pierced into his soul. "Is there anything else you are in need of, Miss Lincoln? Or shall I be on my way?"

"Y-yes, if I could but speak with you for just a moment?" she stammered.

He drew in a deep calming breath. There was no need for him to treat her in such a way, even if she was toying with him. He could rise above, as he always did.

He nodded for her to proceed.

"I merely wished to discuss what occurred the night of the ball."

"Is there really a need? I rather think—"

"Mr. Carter proposed to me."

He blinked, shocked into silence. Mr. Carter, propose? Surely, she was in jest.

Then again, Miss Lincoln and Mr. Carter were very nearly the same person. And if they *were* to marry, then her words at the ball made perfect sense. Of course she would want to remove any thought of matrimony from Benjamin's mind if she was already determined to marry Mr. Carter.

"I see," he said. "Well, I…I trust the two of you will be very happy together."

Had his words sounded as false as they felt? It wasn't his fault he didn't sound sincere. He was far too preoccupied with stopping himself from envisioning Miss Lincoln wrapped up in *that* man's arms.

Miss Lincoln was silent for a moment. "I would hope that you trust in my judgment a little more than for me to accept a proposal from him, sir."

He narrowed his eyes. "You mean you refused him?"

"I did. And had his proposal been in earnest, I *still* would have refused him."

He frowned. "In earnest? What do you mean?"

"Surely you must have noticed how he smelled of drink at the ball. He was rejected by another woman and sought solace with me."

His mind tried to wrap around the information, but confusion still swirled within him.

"You see," she continued, "the words I spoke that night, about wishing to remain single like Aunt Harriet. They were purely for Mr. Carter's benefit. He would not take no for an answer, and I…I did not wish to injure him as I once injured you."

She spoke the truth. Benjamin could not deny it. But how was that to make him feel any better? She very well could have said them for Benjamin's benefit, as well.

Even if she hadn't, he could not allow himself to hope otherwise.

He strapped the barriers once more round his heart and squared his shoulders. "Thank you for explaining, Miss Lincoln. Is there anything else you wish to discuss, or may I take my leave now?"

She stared up at him, wide-eyed and vulnerable. He'd known she'd been attempting to share her feelings with him, but he did not want to hear them. Not now, not ever. Not when he wasn't going to accept them.

Not when he couldn't trust her.

"No, there's nothing more I wish to say," she said, backing away slowly. "I am sorry for wasting your time, Dr. Kent."

She turned away, hanging her head as she moved to the door.

Benjamin clenched his teeth. He would not speak. He would not bring her back. Not while he was finally free.

But his tongue had a mind of its own. "You said your heart ached," he blurted out.

She faced him again in silence.

"Have you…" He swallowed. "Have you any knowledge as to why it might feel so pained?"

She stared up at him, the truth so obvious in her eyes, he wanted to reach out to her. But fear grappled within him. "I have an idea," she whispered. "But…but perhaps you might listen to my heartbeat to see for yourself."

Every logical bone in his body told him to keep away from the siren, to leave her home and person behind forever. But he found his head nodding of its own accord, and soon, the two of them were sitting side by side on the settee.

Clearly, he'd gone mad. Mad for remaining there. Mad for giving in to whatever game she played. Mad for thinking he had power over her.

There was no ailment of the heart that could be solved or diagnosed merely by listening to her pulse. And yet, there he was, doing exactly that.

She shifted toward him, her knee pressing into his.

His heart struggled to beat rhythmically, skipping beats then lurching forward as he reached forth with his right hand, softly pressing his fingers against her neck, just below her jawline.

The energy charging between them grew tenfold as memories of their kiss flooded his mind.

*Listen to her heartbeat. Feel its thrumming swiftly against your finger.*

Tap. Tap. Tap.

Brown eyes.

Tap. Tap.

Rosy cheeks.

Tap.

Red lips.

His eyes were moving on their own, traveling across the beauty of her face.

"Can you feel it?" she whispered. Did she refer to her heart raging or his own? "Can you see why it aches?"

He could. But he wouldn't.

He withdrew his hand and shifted away from the touch of her knee. "I hear nothing abject in your heart's beating at all, Miss Lincoln."

He made to stand, but her soft hand on his arm stopped him. "Dr. Kent," she began.

He shook his head. "I…I can't, Miss Lincoln."

"I know why you do not listen to me," she rushed on. "I know why you do not wish to entrust me once more with your heart. But I beg of you to allow me the chance to prove to you that my feelings for you are in earnest."

His breathing grew labored, as if he'd just run for her at the Frost Fair to save her all over again. Only this time, he was the one in danger. He was the one who was slipping on the ice. He was the one hovering over the raging Thames.

Should he accept her hand and risk the fall? Should he entrust her with his safety?

Or should he look after himself and keep his heart forever guarded —forever safe?

Gently, he pulled away from her touch, standing from the settee. He longed to look at her, but one glance would surely be his undoing.

"I'm sorry, Miss Lincoln," he whispered.

Silence followed until the rustling of her skirts against the settee signaled her standing, as well. "I understand, Dr. Kent. Truly, I do."

Her words were as soft as a whispered breeze, but they nearly knocked him to his knees. "I would find it hard to trust myself after everything we've been through." Her footsteps padded away from him. "I will leave you now. And I shan't bother you again."

She moved farther away. The blood rushed in his ears, and his heart ached as greatly as it did four years ago.

Flashes of the past—of her laughter at his proposal, her refusal—were soon replaced with her apology at Christmas, their laughter while playing games, their speaking of their deepest desires.

Their shared kiss.

Benjamin could bear it no longer. He spun toward her, marching after her with a determined stride and stretching out just before she reached the door.

He clutched her arm in his hand, spinning her toward him and grasping her upper arms.

"I can't," he said through clenched teeth, logic and love fighting a battle in his heart. "Can you not see? I cannot do this!"

She didn't respond, her eyes glistening with tears as she nodded in silence.

"I cannot marry you. I cannot allow myself to fall in love with you again, to believe in your words. Not when...not when my heart has never fully recovered."

She nodded, her voice breaking. "I know. And I should not be asking you to do so again. But I love you, Benjamin."

The words sent a jolt of energy pulsing through every inch of his body. It was true. He'd known it was true every time he met her gaze, saw the truth in her eyes.

"I can't," he whispered, his grip lessening on her arms, his words less forceful. "I can't..."

Or could he?

Slowly, his defenses fell one-by-one, his heart opening to finally hear her words. She loved him. Miss Lucy Lincoln loved him.

His hands slid up her arms and the sides of her neck, resting just below her ears. Her pulse raced, just like before—just like his. The soft trilling encouraged him, invited him to draw closer, so much so that he could no longer resist.

He pressed his lips on hers, and warmth infused his very soul. His hope mingled with his fears, just like the old friends they were, but as each moment passed by, his love for the woman he held in his arms shone brighter and brighter until the fear was snuffed out.

Her hands slipped under his jacket, wrapping around his waist, fingers splayed against the back of his waistcoat. She returned his kiss with fervor, signifying the truth in her declaration of love.

He wanted their kiss to last forever, to allow their lips to increase the bond growing between them that he never knew could be possible.

But she'd expressed her love, and it was now time for him to do the same.

Relief and love spilled forth from Lucy's heart. How grateful she was that she'd pushed through. How grateful she was that Dr. Kent had entrusted his heart with her!

Or…had he?

She could feel his affection for her in his kiss, the way he held her face so gently between his hands, as if he feared she might slip away from him. But had she proven herself worthy of his love, his trust?

Eventually, his kisses slowed, and he pulled away, his breathing ragged as he stared down at her. "I love you," he whispered. "I have never stopped loving you."

She smiled, tears welling in her eyes once again.

"But…" He paused. "I'm afraid. Afraid of losing you again. Afraid that a life with me, the dull physician, will not be exciting enough for you."

Lucy sobered at once, knowing she was the cause of his insecurities. She'd been the one to reject him, to be cruel to him. But it was time to set the record straight.

She reached up, placing a hand against his cheek. "I love you,

Benjamin Kent. *You.* I don't want a life filled with recklessness and risking my life day in and day out. Although, I wouldn't mind you saving me now and again."

His lips lifted at her teasing.

"You are the one I want," she continued. "A life with you is what I desire. I was deceived by Aunt's false happiness, by Mr. Carter's incessant teasing, and by my own selfish desires. But being with you, I see things clearly. I want a simple life. A loving marriage. A home filled with happiness. You, not be enough for me?" She shook her head. "Benjamin, you are everything to me."

Finally—*finally*—the fear fled from his eyes, moisture replacing the emotion as he smiled. "Then dare I ask again, Lucy Lincoln? Will you marry this poor apothecary's son?"

She struggled to grasp a deep breath, so full was her joy. "Yes, Benjamin. I will marry you."

His lips covered hers once more, and nothing else was spoken as the two shared an affection that said far more than any words ever could.

# EPILOGUE

*L*ucy had no notion that winter in Cornwall would be so bitterly cold. The frigid wind from the sea seeped deeper into her bones than any frigid drafts in London ever had, no matter the number of layers she wore.

Even still, she couldn't help but smile as she stood at the edge of the small property her husband had purchased over two months ago, staring at the stormy waves wreaking havoc upon the rocky shores below.

How she loved her new life—as cold as she was. For she had Benjamin to keep her warm.

"I knew I'd find you out here."

As if appearing from her thoughts, Benjamin slipped his arms around her from behind, cradling her in his hold. "You'll catch a cold if you remain out here for too long."

"Thank heavens I know a physician who can nurse me back to health."

"Do you? I happen to know your regular physician is far too busy with his other patients to deal with the likes of headstrong women who don't know the first thing about taking care of themselves."

She laughed, turning in his arms to swat him against his chest. "I'd best be your first patient, sir."

He smiled down at her, kissing the tip of her nose. "You know you are."

She narrowed her eyes playfully. "And I can see past your fibs. You are not nearly as busy as you were in London. You have half as many people to treat."

"Shh. We wouldn't want people to know I've any moment to spare. That would mean less time with my lovely wife."

He stared down at her as the cold wind whipped around them, but when his lips met hers, the freezing air was all but forgotten.

It had been a swift, blissful ten months of marriage they'd shared together thus far. And she knew the rest would be just as glorious. How could it not be, with this man by her side for the rest of it?

Benjamin pulled back after a moment, peering down at her and smoothing the curls away from her brow, though the wind returned it swiftly to her forehead.

"Come. Let us warm up indoors. Your parents will be wondering where we've gone to."

Lucy accepted Benjamin's hand and followed him inside to where Mama and Papa awaited them.

Her parents had visited Lucy's small home twice that year already, and Benjamin's parents had done so once a few months ago. Lucy enjoyed the time they got to spend together. Though, there was one person who had yet to visit, one person whom she feared never would.

That evening, as she sat down to dinner with her parents and husband, enjoying a meal consisting of their leftover Christmas feast, Lucy leaned closer to her mother.

"How is Aunt Harriet?" she asked carefully.

Dr. Kent and Father both felt the same way about the woman, though they were too kind to ever say anything in the contrary.

Mama sighed. "She is well, my dear. I believe she misses you."

Lucy's smile faltered. She missed Aunt Harriet, as well.

After Lucy married, Aunt Harriet, who still lived in London, had hired a young woman to be her companion, no doubt replacing Lucy as Lucy had once replaced Aunt's sister.

She was disappointed that Aunt still had not accepted her marriage to Benjamin—or their move away from London—but Lucy had faith that one day, all would be well with her.

Until then, Lucy would be happy with her choices. For how could she ever regret marrying the man who'd made her happier than she'd ever been?

Benjamin heard his wife ask after Aunt Harriet again, his heart reaching out to her. He knew how she missed her aunt. He'd done everything in his power to receive that woman's approval, but there was nothing more to be done. Still, he had hope that one day, the woman would come around to their marriage—if only for Lucy's sake.

After dinner, the four of them retired to the small sitting room of their modest home. It was not large, by any means, but the house was big enough to grow into and open enough to entertain—though not so large that they would be able to host enormous parties, much to Benjamin's delight.

Still, he encouraged Lucy to entertain as often as she liked, and he promised to be there for her, whether it was to listen to her ramble around strangers or to put on a good face and pretend that he liked socializing. Because he would do anything for his wife.

"How is Fawsley?" Lucy asked as they settled in for hot tea before the fire—the only remedy for cold, Cornish winters.

The house was terribly drafty, but shawls were thrown over the women, and the fireplace did more than enough to keep them all warm.

"The same as it's always been," Mrs. Lincoln responded. "You two are still the talk of the town."

Lucy and Benjamin shared a smile. Their wedding was held months ago in Fawsley, and half the town had shown up specifically to see it occur, for no one ever thought it would happen.

In truth, Benjamin had been afraid it wouldn't have, either. Not because he didn't trust Lucy—for he did with his very heart. What he didn't trust was that something so wonderfully joyous could happen to him. And yet, happen, it did.

His parents had been ecstatic, and still, they wrote them every month with updates to the apothecary shop. Lucy had insisted they continue sending regular funds to Benjamin's father, rather than using any extra money to furnish her new home.

In return, Benjamin's mother would respond with gratitude, never ending a correspondence without asking when she would be receiving grandchildren of her own.

"All in good time," Benjamin would always respond in his letters.

He and Lucy were very much looking forward to starting a family of their own. But as of right now, they were content to settle into their new home, first.

"Martin Carter showed up in Fawsley a few nights before we left," Mrs. Lincoln continued, breaking into Benjamin's thoughts. "Apparently, he's had a change of heart and wishes to be near his family for Christmas this year."

"Who could blame him, after what occurred last Christmas in London?" Lucy said.

"You mean your rejecting him?" Benjamin teased.

Lucy sent him a frown that appeared all too insincere. "No, I was referring, of course, to Miss Robins rejecting him. Besides, you know Mr. Carter's proposal to me was not sincere in the slightest."

Fortunately, Benjamin did know that now. Upon hearing of Lucy and Benjamin becoming engaged, Mr. Carter had expressed his sincerest desires for their happiness, as well as his sincerest apology to Lucy for having proposed while drunken.

"Is he so very miserable still?" Lucy asked her parents.

"All broken hearts mend eventually," Mr. Lincoln said. "Just ask your own husband here."

"Father," Lucy said with widened eyes, but Benjamin merely chuckled.

"It is true. Fortunately, mine was able to be mended by the very woman who broke it. Thank heavens she had the right tools."

"Kind words, kisses…" Mr. Lincoln said.

Lucy buried her head in her hands, and Mrs. Lincoln tutted. "All right, you two. Enough teasing your poor daughter and wife."

Benjamin winked at Lucy, and she smiled in return when she finally lifted her gaze.

That night, as Benjamin and Lucy retired, he wrapped his arms around her from behind, whispering into her ear. "Did you have a pleasant St. Stephen's Day, my love?"

She hummed. "Indeed. And you?"

"I always do when I compare it to what occurred on the second day of Christmas five years ago."

Her pointed elbow jabbed into his side, and he chuckled, holding her all the tighter. "You know I only jest."

"Yes, as usual. Had I known you'd tease me so much about it, I never would've rejected you in the first place."

He breathed in the floral scent of her hair as they fell into silence. "I love you. And I'm so grateful you reconsidered."

She nestled closer to him, leaning her head toward him so he kissed her cheek. "And I'm so very grateful you allowed me to mend your heart."

And mend his heart, she had, with a love as true as he could have ever desired. For it was a love that would never again be torn apart by the world. A love that only grew stronger with time. A love that was born at the Frost Fair.

And how could a love not last with a new beginning such as that?

## THE END

**Read the next book in the Belles of Christmas: Frost Fair series:**
The Christmas Foundling by Martha Keyes

# AUTHOR'S NOTE

One of my favorite ways to end my books is to include a personal note from me to you, my readers. I'm not sure how many of you actually take the time to read the information provided here, but I'm always glad you do—as all authors are!

I strive my very best to provide accurate content without compromising the story, and I can only hope I succeed! If you're interested in learning more about the history involved in *On the Second Day of Christmas*, below is a list of various historical facts I felt were most pressing to address. I hope you find them as fascinating as I did!

First off, let's discuss the Frost Fair. Yes, it was an actual event that took place in London. Although, for the sake of our series—and to make Christmas a little more thrilling—we decided to shift all of the historical facts about the fair to December, instead of when it originally took place in February of 1814.

Another fun fact about the fair: a man and "two lads" did actually float down the Thames on a slab of ice that had broken off! Obviously, I embellished the story to add my own characters and my own spin, but the three were saved in actuality at Billingsgate Bridge by a boatsman.

With Dr. Kent being a physician, I was required to do a lot of research about doctoring at the time. I used many contemporary sources (including one published in 1813) for most of my information used during the fevers and various injuries in this novel.

Other random things I learned: stethoscopes weren't invented or widely used until well after 1816, and there were several sources I read that said physicians would sometimes listen to heartbeats and lungs by pressing their ears against the patients backs or chests. As with everything, medical practices varied between physicians, but more often than not, physicians did not do much handling of the patients at all, whereas surgeons did. There were some exceptions, of course, and I made Dr. Kent one of those exceptions.

As authors, the amount of research and thought we put into our stories borders on, well, crazy. The time it takes and the effort involved to ensure one sentence is historically accurate is also insane. For example: Dr. Kent coming to examine Lucy for the last time in Aunt Harriet's dressing room. I had to research for hours where they would actually meet that was proper, now that she was no longer bedridden. I used *Sense and Sensibility* as my research, for when Jane Austen wrote that Colonel Brandon met with Marianne, she had them go to Mrs. Palmer's dressing room instead of elsewhere.

Trying to search for a novel Mr. Lincoln would enjoy was just as difficult for me as it was for Lucy and Benjamin to find one. When I finally settled on *The Life of Nelson,* I wanted to get an accurate description. Imagine my delight when I found online an actual first edition of the book! It was a bit pricey, but from pictures, I was able to get a fairly accurate description, and I hope I was able to convey that in my own writing!

Finally, I'm sure you've all noticed that it's a running joke now for me to put Cornwall somehow in each of my books. If I can't write a book solely in Cornwall, I'll keep adding it into my stories in any way I can. It might be fun for you as a reader to keep your eyes open in the future—because I'll always mention Cornwall in my later books!

Now, if you enjoyed "On the Second Day of Christmas," please consider leaving a review. And if you'd like to receive the latest news about my future novels, sign up for my newsletter. I always share newly released and discounted clean romance novels, as well as fun polls, quotes, and giveaways. My newsletter subscribers are also the first to see sneak peeks and cover reveals!

Make sure to follow me on Facebook (for more clean romance deals) and Instagram (for photos of my travels to the UK and more).

I hope to connect with you soon!

Deborah

# ACKNOWLEDGMENTS

Are these acknowledgements starting to sound all the same? I can't help it! There are too many people I need to thank for their help. Maybe I'll switch it up today by thanking my husband first. Will that help matters?

All right, husband. My thanks first and foremost goes to you! Thank you for dealing with my special form of crazy, for supporting me, and for loving me. I owe everything to you. And I kinda love you. A lot.

Thank you so much to Kasey Stockton, Martha Keyes, and Jess Heileman for your help with this book! Oh, and for your help in all matters of my life. Because let's be honest, I need it. I love working with you ladies. Here's to many more years!

A special thanks must go to Martha Keyes again, for not only did she suggest a number of medical books for me to research, but she also helped me with the questions I couldn't find the answers to. Because of that, she received a special mention in this book by showing up as Lucy's servant. Maybe if you keep up the good work, Martha, you'll graduate one day to something other than a lady's maid.

Thanks to the Belles of Christmas authors, Ashtyn Newbold, Kasey Stockton, Mindy Burbidge Strunk, and Martha Keyes. It is so fun working with you all, brainstorming together, and creating this series! Thank you so much for all the laughs that kept me sane this year.

As always, I need to thank my editor, Jenny. I've used you since the beginning, and you've helped me with almost every story I've written. Thank you!

Lastly, I'm going to surprise you all by thanking…Cornwall. "What?" you may be asking yourselves. "Why is she writing thank you to Cornwall? The majority of this book isn't even *in* Cornwall…" Well, as I'm sure many of you know, I'm obsessed with that place. I didn't get to go this past year (yet another disappointment of COVID), but the memory of my time there, photos I've looked at, and this epilogue I somehow finagled into being in Cornwall have helped me through more than I can ever say. I can't wait to go there again. So yes, thank you, Cornwall for being the one place where I can be the real "me."

# BOOKS BY DEBORAH M. HATHAWAY

Stand Alone Novels

A Secret Fire

When Two Rivers Meet

To Warm a Wintered Heart

*A Cornish Romance Series*

On the Shores of Tregalwen, a Novella

Behind the Light of Golowduyn, Book One

For the Lady of Lowena, Book Two

Near the Ruins of Penharrow, Book Three

*Belles of Christmas Multi-Author Series*

Nine Ladies Dancing, Book Four

On the Second Day of Christmas, Book Four

*Seasons of Change Multi-Author Series*

The Cottage by Coniston, Book Five

# ABOUT THE AUTHOR

 Deborah M. Hathaway graduated from Utah State University with a BA in English, Creative Writing. As a young girl, she devoured Jane Austen's novels while watching and re-watching every adaptation of Pride & Prejudice she could, entirely captured by all things Regency and romance.

Throughout her early life, she wrote many short stories, poems, and essays, but it was not until after her marriage that she was finally able to complete her first romance novel, attributing the completion to her courtship with, and love of, her charming, English husband. Deborah finds her inspiration for her novels in her everyday experiences with her husband and children and during her travels to the United Kingdom, where she draws on the beauty of the country in such places as Ireland, Yorkshire, and her beloved Cornwall.

Made in the USA
Columbia, SC
02 July 2023